BOOKWORMS CLUB
Gold

STORIES FOR READING CIRCLES
Stage 3 (1000 headwords)
Stage 4 (1400 headwords)

The seven short stories in this book come from different volumes in the Oxford Bookworms Library. There are five stories at Stage 3 and two stories at Stage 4. All have been specially chosen for Reading Circles.

There are many different kinds of story in this book. If you want to feel afraid, try a classic ghost story by M. R. James, or a chilling horror story by Edgar Allan Poe. What does a lonely, unloved child do in the house of his hated aunt? Saki's story will tell you. And as Dunstan Thwaite plans the perfect murder, you begin to see how easily the plan could go horribly wrong. For true love, you can follow the lives of Cora and Baptista. For Cora, it is a dark and stormy road indeed; for Baptista, it is a strange path but in the end not a sad one. And Arthur C. Clarke will take you into the future, where life on the Moon brings problems no one has ever dreamed of . . .

OXFORD BOOKWORMS LIBRARY
Series Editor: Jennifer Bassett
Founder Editor: Tricia Hedge

YDD Diggg >> I'M DEEZy D

BOOKWORMS CLUB
Gold

STORIES FOR READING CIRCLES

Editor:
Mark Furr

OXFORD UNIVERSITY PRESS

OXFORD
UNIVERSITY PRESS

Great Clarendon Street, Oxford OX2 6DP

Oxford University Press is a department of the University of Oxford.
It furthers the University's objective of excellence in research, scholarship,
and education by publishing worldwide in

Oxford New York

Auckland Cape Town Dar es Salaam Hong Kong Karachi
Kuala Lumpur Madrid Melbourne Mexico City Nairobi
New Delhi Shanghai Taipei Toronto

With offices in

Argentina Austria Brazil Chile Czech Republic France Greece
Guatemala Hungary Italy Japan Poland Portugal Singapore
South Korea Switzerland Thailand Turkey Ukraine Vietnam

OXFORD and OXFORD ENGLISH are registered trade marks of
Oxford University Press in the UK and in certain other countries

ISBN 978 0 19 472002 1

Printed in Hong Kong

ACKNOWLEDGEMENTS
The publishers are grateful to the following
for their kind permission to adapt copyright material:
Pollinger Limited and Evensford Productions Ltd for *The Daffodil Sky*;
The Society of Authors as the Literary Representative of the Estate of Freeman Wills Crofts
for *The Railway Crossing*, which was originally published as *The Level Crossing*;
Gollancz for *The Secret*, originally published in Arthur C. Clarke's *The Collected Stories*

PUPBLISHER'S NOTE
The story entitled *A Moment of Madness* was published in its
original version by Thomas Hardy under the title *A Mere Interlude*

CONTENTS

SOURCE OF STORIES

The seven stories in this book were originally published in different volumes in the OXFORD BOOKWORMS LIBRARY. They appeared in the following titles:

The Black Cat
Edgar Allan Poe, from *Tales of Mystery and Imagination*
Retold by Margaret Naudi

Sredni Vashtar
Saki, from *Tooth and Claw*
Retold by Rosemary Border

The Railway Crossing
Freeman Wills Crofts, from *As the Inspector Said and Other Stories*
Retold by John Escott

The Daffodil Sky
H. E. Bates, from *Go, Lovely Rose and Other Stories*
Retold by Rosemary Border

A Moment of Madness
Thomas Hardy, from *The Three Strangers and Other Stories*
Retold by Clare West

The Secret
Arthur C. Clarke, from *The Songs of Distant Earth and Other Stories*
Retold by Jennifer Bassett

The Experiment
M. R. James, from *The Unquiet Grave*
Retold by Peter Hawkins

~

Welcome
to Reading Circles

Reading Circles are small groups of students who meet in the classroom to talk about stories. Each student has a special role, and usually there are six roles in the Circle:

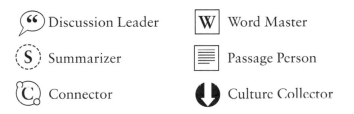

💬 Discussion Leader	W Word Master
S Summarizer	▤ Passage Person
C Connector	⬇ Culture Collector

Each role has a role sheet with notes and questions which will help you prepare for your Reading Circle discussions in the classroom. You can read more about the roles and the role sheets on pages 99 to 105 at the back of this book.

The stories in this book have been specially chosen for Reading Circles. They have many different themes, and students everywhere enjoy reading them and talking about them in their Circle. Everybody's ideas are important; there are no 'right' or 'wrong' answers when you are talking about stories.

Enjoy the reading, enjoy the talking – and discover the magic of Reading Circles . . .

Mark Furr
Hawaii, May 2006

The Black Cat

~

Most people, once or twice in their lives, do bad things that they feel ashamed of afterwards. Perhaps it is something stupid or unkind . . . even cruel, or hateful. A few people go beyond this, and do things so evil, so violent, so terrible, that the rest of the world turns away from them in horror.

These are the people who walk on the dark side of life – like the man who tells this story, a man who was once quiet and gentle, a man who loved animals deeply, especially his black cat Pluto . . .

EDGAR ALLAN POE

The Black Cat

Retold by Margaret Naudi

I know you will not believe this story. Only a madman could hope that you would believe it – and I am not mad. But as I am going to die tomorrow, I would like to tell my story to the world today. Perhaps some day, somebody more calm and less excitable than me will be able to explain it.

I have always loved animals. I loved them deeply, from the very first days of my life. When I was young, we always had many animals in our house, and so I used to spend most of my days playing with them and taking care of them. As the years passed, I grew into a quiet, gentle man, and my love for animals grew too. I found that they were more friendly, more honest than most men. Animals were always my best friends.

I got married when I was quite young. Luckily, my wife loved animals too, and she used to buy me many animals as presents. In fact, our house was always full of animals – we had birds, fish, a dog, chickens, and *a cat*.

This cat, whom we called Pluto, was a large black cat. He was a beautiful animal, and he was also very clever. I loved Pluto more than I loved all my other animals. I wanted to do everything for him myself, so I never let my wife take care of him. I used to play with him and give him his food, and he followed me everywhere I went.

For several years Pluto and I were the best of friends, but during this time my life slowly changed. I became a heavy drinker, and my need for alcohol soon grew into a terrible disease. I was often angry and violent. I began to shout at my wife, and I even started to hit her. My animals, too, felt the change in me. I stopped taking care of them and sometimes I was even cruel to them. But I was never cruel to Pluto. As time passed, my disease grew worse, and soon even Pluto was not safe from my violence.

One night I arrived home late. I was very, very drunk. When Pluto saw me, he tried to run away from me, and this made me angry. I caught him by his neck and shook him. He, in his fright, bit me on the hand. At once, a wild, terrible anger filled me, and I could feel nothing except burning hate. Slowly I took a knife from my pocket, opened it, and then carefully cut out one of Pluto's eyes from its socket. I shake today as I write these words down. Every time I remember that day, I still feel sadness and pain.

When I woke up the next morning, I felt ashamed of what I had done. But this feeling was not strong enough to make me change my life. I continued to drink because it was too difficult for me to stop. Soon, I had forgotten what I had done.

As the months passed, Pluto got better. His empty eye socket still looked terrible, but at least he wasn't in pain any more. Not surprisingly, he used to run away from me when he saw me, frightened that I would hurt him again. At first I was sad to see him run away – an animal which had once so loved me. Then I began to feel a little angry. There is something strange about the human heart. We humans seem to like hurting ourselves. Haven't we all, a hundred times, done something stupid or evil just because we know that we should not do it? It was because of this, this need to hurt myself, that I did this next evil thing . . .

One morning I woke, found a rope and calmly tied it round Pluto's neck. Then I hung the poor animal from a tree and left it there to die. I cried as I did this terrible thing. My face was wet with tears and my heart was black and heavy. But I killed it. I killed it *because* I knew it had loved me, *because* it hadn't hurt me, even *because* I knew that I was doing something terrible and wrong.

That same night we had a fire in our house. I was woken from my sleep by loud shouts of 'Fire!' When I opened my eyes, I found that the fire had already reached the bedroom. My wife and I ran out of the house as fast as we could. Luckily we escaped death, but the house and almost everything in it was destroyed.

The next day I went back into the house and saw several people standing in a group, looking at a wall. It was the only wall of the house that was still standing after the fire. It was one of my bedroom walls, the one where the head of my bed had rested. As I came nearer to the wall I heard someone say, 'How strange!' and another person, 'That's impossible!' And then I saw it – a huge cat. Not a real cat, but the shape of a cat outlined in the white bedroom wall. It was as clear as a picture. I could even see a rope around the animal's neck.

I stood there in horror, too frightened to move. Then, slowly, I thought back to the night before. I had left the cat hanging from a tree, in the garden at the back of my house. When a neighbour had first noticed the fire, many people had run into the garden. One of them had probably cut the cat from the tree and thrown it through my open window, in order to wake me up. The cat's body had hit my bedroom wall and left its shape there, because the plaster on that wall was new and still soft.

Although I thought that this was a very reasonable explanation, the strange shape on the wall still worried me. I thought about the cat day and night. I began to feel sorry that I had killed it. I started walking around the streets at night looking at all the cats, to see if I could find another one like Pluto.

One night, I was drinking in my favourite bar when I suddenly noticed a large, black cat. I went up to it and touched it. It was very large – as large as Pluto had been. It also looked very like Pluto. Except for one thing. Pluto had been black all over, but this cat had a white mark on its front.

I touched the cat and he immediately lay down against my leg and seemed very friendly towards me. This, I decided, was the cat that I wanted. I offered the barman some money to buy the cat from him, but he said that the cat didn't belong to him. In fact, he had no idea where it had come from.

So I took the cat home. My wife liked it immediately, and it stayed with us from that day. But soon – I do not know why – the cat started to make me angry, and, as time passed, I began to hate it. I did not hurt it in any way, but I always tried to keep as far away from it as possible.

I knew one reason why I hated this cat so much. On the morning after I had brought it home, I saw that, like Pluto, it had lost one of its eyes. My wife, who was the kind, gentle person that I had once been, only loved the cat more because of this. But the cat didn't like my wife. It loved me alone.

Every time I sat down, it used to jump onto my knees. When I went out of a room, it used to run out in front of me and get between my feet, or climb up my legs. At these times, I wanted to kill it. But I didn't, because I was too afraid – afraid of the cat, and even more afraid of the white mark on its chest.

I have already mentioned this mark. At first, there was nothing strange about it. It was just a white mark. But slowly this mark grew and changed until it had the clear shape of a terrible, a horrible thing – I find it difficult, here in my prison, to write the word. It was the shape of the GALLOWS! Yes, those horrible wooden posts from which they hang men by a rope around the neck!

As each day passed, my fear grew and grew. I, a man, a strong man, had become afraid of a cat! Why was I so frightened, so worried by a stupid animal? Day and night, I could get no rest. I had the most terrible dreams, and my mind turned to dark, evil thoughts. I hated everything, everybody – and life itself.

One day my wife and I needed to get something from

the cellar underneath the house. The cat followed us down the steps and threw itself in front of me. I almost fell on my face and, mad with anger, I took hold of an axe and tried to kill the animal. But my wife caught my arm to stop me, and then anger exploded in my mind. I turned and drove the axe deep into her head. She fell dead on the floor, without a sound.

After this horrible murder, I calmly made plans to hide the body. I knew I couldn't take it out of the house, either by day or night, because the neighbours would see me. So I had to think of other ways . . . I could cut the body up into very small pieces and then burn them in a fire. I could hide the body under the floor. Or I could put the body in a box and then ask someone to carry the box away . . . Finally, I thought of a better idea. I decided to hide the body behind the walls of the cellar.

I knew immediately which wall to choose. There was a wall in the cellar round the bottom of an old chimney, which was no longer used. This wall had bricks in the front and back but was empty in the middle. I started work at once. I took out some of the bricks from the front wall and carefully put the body against the back wall. Then I put back the bricks and covered them with plaster. I made sure that the plaster did not look new, and soon the wall looked just the same as all the other walls. When I had finished my work, I looked at the plaster. 'I've never done a better piece of work!' I said to myself happily.

I then looked around for the cat, to kill it. It had brought too much unhappiness into my life, and so it, too, must now die. I looked for it everywhere, but it had disappeared. I was free at last! That night I had a deep, peaceful sleep – I, who had just killed my wife, slept well!

Three days passed and still the cat did not appear. I was now a happy man, happier than I had been for a long time. I wasn't worried by what I had done. People had asked a few questions and the police had visited my house, but they had found nothing.

On the fourth day the police visited again and began to search the house. They looked into all the rooms and then went down into the cellar. I went with them, feeling calm and safe. I watched them as they looked everywhere. They seemed quite happy that there was nothing there and they got ready to leave. I was very happy. I was sure that I was safe, but I wanted to say something, just a word or two, to show how unworried I was.

'Gentlemen,' I said, 'I'm pleased that you've found nothing here, and that you are now leaving this house . . . But let me show you something, gentlemen. Do you see how well built this house is? These walls, you will notice, are very strong.' As I said these words, I knocked on the wall with a stick – the wall where I had hidden my wife!

At that moment we heard a sound. It was a strange sound, unlike anything I had ever heard before. The sound was soft at first, almost like a baby crying. Then it grew louder and louder and turned into one long, endless scream. It was like a cry rising from Hell.

The policemen looked at me, then at one another. They ran to the wall and started pulling out the bricks as fast as they could. In minutes the wall was down and there, for all to see, was the body of my dead wife. On top of her head, with a red, open mouth and one burning eye, sat the black cat – the animal which had made me a murderer, and which would now send me to my death.

I had put the horrible thing into the wall, alive, with my wife!

WORD FOCUS

Match each word with an appropriate meaning. Then use seven of the thirteen words to complete the passage below. (Use one word in each gap.) Who is the person telling the story in the passage?

alcohol	with a sick mind
axe	a room in the ground under a house
bricks	not kind; bringing pain or trouble to someone
cellar	very bad, very wrong
chest	the place where bad people go when they die
cruel	the front part of the top of the body
evil	making you very frightened
hell	a tool for cutting trees and wood
horrible	the hole in the head where the eye is
mad	showing the line or shape of something
outlined	small hard blocks that are used for building walls
plaster	liquid in drinks like beer and whisky that can make people drunk
socket	something soft and wet which is put over bricks and which hardens to make the wall flat and straight

'. . . Then we went down to the _____. And we found nothing there. But when we were leaving, the man hit the wall with a stick. And suddenly, we heard a soft sound, but soon it grew louder and was like a cry rising from _____! We ran to the wall and started pulling out the _____. Inside the wall, we saw something _____ – the body of the man's wife. And sitting on her head was a black cat with a strange mark on its _____ and one empty eye _____. Next to the body, we found a weapon, a bloody _____.'

STORY FOCUS 1

In a story, the narrator is a character who tells the story. What do you think about the narrator of *The Black Cat*? Choose one of these adjectives for the first gap in each sentence, and then write as much as you like to finish the sentences.

angry, calm, careful, clever, cruel, evil, gentle, horrible, kind, mad, nervous, violent

1 I think the narrator was _____ because _____.
2 The narrator was _____ when _____.
3 The narrator wasn't _____ when _____.
4 When the narrator hung the cat, he was _____ because _____.
5 After he killed his wife, the narrator was _____ because _____.

STORY FOCUS 2

Match these halves of sentences to make a paragraph of five sentences. Who do you think the narrator is here?

1 The man was my best friend . . .
2 For several years, the man was kind, . . .
3 At first, the man was cruel to the other animals, . . .
4 Then, one night, I tried to run away from him, . . .
5 Finally, he took a knife from his pocket, . . .

6 . . . but the man caught me and shook me by the neck.
7 . . . but he wasn't cruel to me.
8 . . . because he gave me my food and played with me every day.
9 . . . but then the man's life slowly changed.
10 . . . and he cut my eye out of its socket.

Sredni Vashtar

~

Children can live in two different worlds at the
same time. One is the real, boring, everyday world,
and the other is a world where you are king of
your country, where your best friend lives on the
moon, where you can eat hot buttered toast all
day long . . .

Conradin lives with his aunt. He is ten years old,
lonely, and often ill. One of Conradin's worlds is the
colourless, comfortless world of his aunt. And the
other is the bright, exciting, violent world of his
imagination, where his unkind aunt has no place,
and where Sredni Vashtar has become his god . . .

Sredni Vashtar

Retold by Rosemary Border

Conradin was ten years old and was often ill.

'The boy is not strong,' said the doctor. 'He will not live much longer.' But the doctor did not know about Conradin's imagination. In Conradin's lonely, loveless world, his imagination was the only thing that kept him alive.

Conradin's parents were dead and he lived with his aunt. The aunt did not like Conradin and was often unkind to him. Conradin hated her with all his heart, but he obeyed her quietly and took his medicine without arguing. Mostly he kept out of her way. She had no place in his world. His real, everyday life in his aunt's colourless, comfortless house was narrow and uninteresting. But inside his small, dark head exciting and violent thoughts ran wild. In the bright world of his imagination Conradin was strong and brave. It was a wonderful world, and the aunt was locked out of it.

The garden was no fun. There was nothing interesting to do. He was forbidden to pick the flowers. He was forbidden to eat the fruit. He was forbidden to play on the grass. But behind some trees, in a forgotten corner of the garden, there was an old shed.

Nobody used the shed, and Conradin took it for his own. To him it became something between a playroom and a church. He filled it with ghosts and animals from his imagination. But there were also two living things in the shed. In one corner lived an old, untidy-looking chicken. Conradin had no people to love, and this chicken was the boy's dearest friend. And in a dark, secret place at the back of the shed was a large wooden box with bars across the front. This was the home of a very large ferret with long, dangerous teeth and claws. Conradin had bought the ferret and its box from a friendly boy, who lived in the village. It had cost him all his money, but Conradin did not mind. He was most terribly afraid of the ferret, but he loved it with all his heart. It was his wonderful, terrible secret. He gave the ferret a strange and beautiful name and it became his god.

The aunt went to church every Sunday. She took Conradin with her, but to Conradin her church and her god were without meaning. They seemed grey and uninteresting. The true god lived in the shed, and his name was Sredni Vashtar.

Every Thursday, in the cool, silent darkness of the shed, Conradin took presents to his god. He took flowers in summer and fruits in autumn, and he made strange and wonderful songs for his god. Sometimes, on days when something important happened, Conradin took special presents. He stole salt from the kitchen and placed it carefully and lovingly in front of the ferret's box.

One day the aunt had the most terrible toothache. It continued for three days. Morning and evening Conradin put salt in front of his god. In the end he almost believed that Sredni Vashtar himself had sent the toothache.

17

After a time the aunt noticed Conradin's visits to the shed.

'It's not good for him to play out there in the cold,' she said. She could always find a reason to stop Conradin enjoying himself. The next morning at breakfast she told Conradin that she had sold the chicken. She looked at Conradin's white face, and waited for him to cry or to be angry. But Conradin said nothing; there was nothing to say.

Perhaps the aunt felt sorry. That afternoon there was hot buttered toast for tea. Toast was usually forbidden. Conradin loved it, but the aunt said that it was bad for him. Also, it made extra work for the cook. Conradin looked at the toast and quietly took a piece of bread and butter.

'I thought you liked toast,' the aunt said crossly.

'Sometimes,' said Conradin.

In the shed that evening Conradin looked sadly at the empty corner where his chicken had lived. And, for the first time, he asked his ferret-god to do something for him.

'Do one thing for me, Sredni Vashtar,' he said softly.

He did not say what he wanted. Sredni Vashtar was a god, after all. There is no need to explain things to gods. Then, with a last look at the empty corner, Conradin returned to the world that he hated.

And every night, in the shed and in his bedroom, Conradin repeated again and again,

'Do one thing for me, Sredni Vashtar.'

So Conradin's visits to the shed continued. The aunt noticed, and went to look in the shed again.

'What are you keeping in that locked box?' she asked.
'I'm sure you're keeping an animal there. It's not good for
you.'

Conradin said nothing.

The aunt searched his bedroom until she found the key
to the box. She marched down to the shed. It was a cold
afternoon, and Conradin was forbidden to go outside. From
the window of the dining-room Conradin could just see the
door of the shed. He stood and waited.

He saw the aunt open the shed door. She went inside.
Now, thought Conradin, she has found the box. She is
opening the door, and feeling about inside the box where
my god lives.

'Do one thing for me, Sredni Vashtar,' said Conradin
softly. But he said it without hope. She will win, he
thought. She always wins. Soon she will come out of the
shed and give her orders. Somebody will come and take my
wonderful god away – not a god any more, just a brown
ferret in a box. Then there will be nothing important in my
life . . . The doctor will be right. I shall sicken and die. She
will win. She always wins . . . In his pain and misery,
Conradin began to sing the song of his god:

> *Sredni Vashtar went into battle. His thoughts*
> *were red thoughts and his teeth were white. His*
> *enemies called for peace but he brought them*
> *death. Sredni Vashtar the Beautiful.*

Suddenly he stopped singing and went nearer to the
window. The door of the shed was still open. Slowly, very
slowly the minutes went by. Conradin watched the birds on

the grass. He counted them, always with one eye on that open door. The unsmiling housekeeper came in with the tea things. Still Conradin stood and watched and waited. Hope was growing, like a small, sick flower, in his heart. Very softly he sang his song again, and his hope grew and grew. And then he saw a very wonderful thing.

Out of the shed came a long, low, yellow-and-brown animal. There were red, wet stains around its mouth and neck.

'Sredni Vashtar!' said Conradin softly. The ferret-god made its way to the bottom of the garden. It stopped for a moment, then went quietly into the long grass and disappeared for ever.

'Tea is ready,' said the housekeeper. 'Where is your aunt?'

'She went down to the shed,' said Conradin.

And, while the housekeeper went down to call the aunt, Conradin took the toasting-fork out of the dining-room cupboard. He sat by the fire and toasted a piece of bread for himself. While he was toasting it and putting butter on it, Conradin listened to the noises beyond the dining-room door. First there were loud screams – that was the housekeeper. Then there was the cook's answering cry. Soon there came the sound of several pairs of feet. They were carrying something heavy into the house.

'Who is going to tell that poor child?' said the housekeeper.

'Well, someone will have to,' answered the cook. And, while they were arguing, Conradin made himself another piece of toast.

WORD FOCUS

Use the clues below and complete this crossword with words from the story.

ACROSS

1 In the garden Conradin was
_____ to pick the flowers, eat
the fruit, and play on the grass.

4 Sredni Vashtar had long sharp
_____ on its feet.

6 Conradin went to _____ with
his aunt every Sunday.

7 After the chicken was sold,
there was hot buttered _____
for tea.

9 Conradin thought that Sredni
Vashtar was a _____.

DOWN

1 Sredni Vashtar was really a
_____, a small but dangerous
animal used for catching rabbits.

2 Conradin's body was weak, but
in the bright world of his _____,
he was strong and brave.

3 Conradin's aunt had a terrible
_____ for three days.

5 Conradin's parents were dead,
so he lived with his _____.

8 Conradin loved to go to the old
_____ in the corner of the garden.

21

STORY FOCUS 1

Here are four new endings for the story. Which do you prefer? Explain why, or write a new ending for the story yourself.

1 Conradin's aunt does not die. She goes to the hospital and gets well. Then she goes home and is very kind to Conradin . . .
2 After his aunt dies, Conradin gets well. He continues to live in the house and grows up to be a strong young man. Of course, Conradin always keeps many animals in the garden . . .
3 Later that night, Sredni Vashtar goes quietly into Conradin's room – and kills the boy while he is sleeping . . .
4 When the housekeeper comes back from the shed, she looks for Conradin. But he isn't in the house. In the boy's chair, by the fire, there is a long, brown animal with dangerous teeth and claws . . .

STORY FOCUS 2

Imagine that you are a detective. You think the death of Conradin's aunt was probably not an accident. But what *did* happen to her? You can ask Conradin five questions to find out what happened to his aunt and why. Which five questions will you ask him?

1
2
3
4
5

The Railway
Crossing

~

What is the perfect crime? Is it a murder when the murderer is never caught? Or perhaps the perfect murder is never reported as a murder at all, because everybody believes it was an accident.

Dunstan Thwaite is a troubled man, a man with a guilty secret, a man with a blackmailer always breathing down his neck, asking for more, and yet more, money. Something must be done. So Thwaite begins to plan – a sleeping powder, the hands of a clock, a passing freight train on the railway . . .

The Railway Crossing

Retold by John Escott

Dunstan Thwaite looked at the railway crossing and decided that it was time for John Dunn to die. It was a very suitable place for a murder. There were trees all around, and they hid the trains which came so fast along the railway line. The nearest house was Thwaite's own, and this was also hidden by the trees. People and traffic did not use the crossing very often, and the big gates were kept locked. There was a small gate used by passengers going to the station, but at night it was always quiet.

Thwaite was a worried man. He had to use sleeping powders to help him sleep. But after tonight, things were going to be different. The time had come to stop the blackmail. The time had come for John Dunn to die.

It all began five years earlier . . .

Thwaite worked in the offices of a large company, and his only money was the money that the company paid him. It was not much, but it was enough. Then he met the beautiful Miss Hilda Lorraine and asked her to marry him.

She came from an important family who were supposed to be very rich, but in fact they had less money than Thwaite had thought. He learned that he would have to pay for the wedding himself. And he did not have enough money for the expensive kind of wedding that Miss Lorraine wanted. So Thwaite stole a thousand pounds, by changing the figures in the company's books. He planned to put the money back after he was married, but someone discovered that it was missing.

Thwaite kept quiet. Another man was thought to be the thief, and he lost his job. Thwaite still said nothing.

But John Dunn worked in the same office. He worked closely with Thwaite and guessed Thwaite's crime. He searched through the company's books until he found what he was looking for. Then he went to Thwaite.

'Sorry to have to ask you, Mr Thwaite,' he said. 'I need a hundred pounds . . . for my son. He's in a bit of trouble, you see . . .'

'But you don't have a son,' said Thwaite.

Dunn just smiled. It wasn't a very nice smile. 'A hundred pounds,' he said again.

And then Thwaite knew that he was being blackmailed.

He paid Dunn one hundred pounds, and Dunn said nothing more for a year. During that time, Thwaite got married.

Then the day came when Dunn asked him for more money.

'Two hundred and fifty pounds,' he said to Thwaite.

'I can't pay—' began Thwaite.

But he did. Either he paid or he went to prison.

It went on for five years, and each time Dunn wanted more money. Thwaite found it difficult to live on the money that he was left with. His wife liked expensive things.

An expensive house, an expensive car, visits to expensive restaurants. She also discovered that some of the money her husband was paid each year seemed to disappear. He tried to lie about it, but he knew that she thought he was paying to keep another woman.

Oh, how he hated John Dunn! Something must happen! And then he remembered the railway crossing.

It was not a new idea. Weeks before, he had thought about what *could* happen there. The idea came when the doctor gave him some powders to help him sleep. He thought about giving Dunn enough of them to kill him, but then he got a better idea. Although he was afraid, Thwaite slowly realized that murder was the only answer to his problem.

Then Dunn asked for more money.

'Five hundred pounds, Mr Thwaite,' Dunn told him.

'Five hundred!' said Thwaite. 'Why not ask for the moon? You'll get neither one nor the other.'

'Five hundred,' repeated Dunn, calmly.

It was then that Thwaite decided to murder the other man. He pretended to think about the money for a moment, then he said, 'Come to my house tomorrow night and we'll talk.' He remembered his wife was going to be away in London all night. 'And bring those papers from the office which you want me to look at.'

'All right,' said Dunn.

The following evening, Thwaite put two hundred pounds in his pocket. Then he put half of one of his sleeping powders into a whisky bottle. There was only enough whisky for two glasses, but there was an unopened bottle next to it. Next he put a hammer into one pocket of his overcoat, and a torch into the other pocket. The coat was outside the door of his study. Lastly, he moved the hands on his watch and on the study clock forward by ten minutes. Those extra ten minutes would give him his alibi.

Thwaite knew that he must be extra careful. He knew that people at the office thought there was some secret between him and Dunn. A secret that Thwaite didn't want anyone to know.

'If Dunn is killed,' he thought, 'they'll wonder if it was really an accident, or if I murdered him.'

But if his plan went well, the police would believe that he hadn't left the house.

Thwaite sat down to wait for John Dunn. He thought about what he was going to do. Murder! He could almost see his hand holding the hammer above Dunn; could hear the awful sound of it crashing down on to the man's head. He could see Dunn's dead body! Dead all except the eyes, which looked at Thwaite . . . followed him everywhere he went . . .

He tried to calm himself. He remembered why he was doing this. When Dunn was dead, his problems were over.

Half an hour later, Dunn arrived. Jane opened the door. Jane was the servant who lived in the house with Thwaite and his wife. She brought Dunn into the study.

Thwaite smiled in a friendly way. 'Oh, good. You've brought those papers for me to see, Dunn. Thank you.'

After Jane left, the two men looked at each other.

'Give me the papers,' Thwaite said. 'I'll look at them now that you've brought them.' Fifteen minutes later, he gave the papers back to Dunn and sat back in his chair. 'Now, about that other matter.' He got up. 'But why not have a drink first?'

'No, thank you,' said Dunn. He looked afraid.

'What are you afraid of?' said Thwaite. He gave Dunn the opened whisky bottle and two glasses. 'We can both drink the same whisky, if you like. Here, you do it.'

After a moment, Dunn put whisky into each glass, then he waited until Thwaite drank before he drank his own. Thwaite watched him. How long before the other man began to feel sleepy? Thwaite needed all of one sleeping powder to make *him* sleep, but Dunn did not usually take them.

'Listen, Dunn,' said Thwaite, 'I haven't got five hundred pounds, but I can give you this.' He took the money from his pocket and put it on the table.

Dunn counted it. 'Two hundred?' he said, with a laugh. 'Are you trying to be funny?'

'I'm not saying it will be the last,' said Thwaite. 'Take it now and be pleased that you've got it.'

Dunn shook his head. 'Five hundred, Mr Thwaite.'

'I've told you, I can't do it,' said Thwaite. 'And I won't do it. You can tell everyone what I did – I don't care any more. It's been five years, and I've done a lot of good work for the company during that time. I saved them a lot more than a thousand pounds. I'll sell this house and pay them back. I'll take my punishment, then I'll go and live in another country and give myself a new name.'

'And your wife?' said Dunn.

'My wife will leave the country first,' Thwaite told him. 'She'll wait for me to come out of prison. It won't be more than two or three years. So you can take the two hundred pounds, or you can do your worst!'

The powder in the whisky was beginning to make Dunn sleepy. He looked stupidly at Thwaite, and Thwaite began to worry. Had he given the other man too much? He looked at the clock. There was not much time left.

'Will you take it, or leave it?' asked Thwaite.

'Five hundred,' said Dunn, in a heavy voice. 'I want five hundred.'

'You can go and do your worst,' said Thwaite.

Dunn held out a shaking hand. 'Come on, pay me.'

Thwaite began to worry again. 'Are you feeling all right, Dunn? Have some more whisky.'

He opened the other bottle and put some whisky in Dunn's glass. Dunn drank it, and it seemed to make him feel better.

'That was strange,' he said. 'I didn't feel very well, but I feel a little better now.'

'If you're going to catch your train, you must go,' said Thwaite. 'Tell me tomorrow what you finally decide to do. Take the two hundred with you.'

Dunn thought for a moment, then picked up the money. He looked at his watch, then looked at the study clock.

'Your clock is wrong,' he said. 'I have ten more minutes.'

'Wrong?' said Thwaite. He looked at his own watch. 'It's your watch that's wrong. Look at mine.'

Dunn looked and seemed unable to understand it. He stood up . . . and almost fell back again.

Thwaite hid a smile. This was how he wanted Dunn to be.

'You're not feeling well,' he said. 'I'll take you to the station. Wait until I get my coat.'

Now that the time was here, Thwaite felt cool and calm.

He put on his coat, feeling the hammer in the pocket, then went back into the study.

'We'll go out this way,' he said.

There was a side door from the study into the garden. Thwaite closed it silently and it locked automatically behind him. It was his plan to return that way, go in quietly again, and then to change the clock and his watch back to the right time. Then he would shout 'Goodnight', and close the front door very loudly, pretending that somebody had left just then. Next, he would call Jane and ask for some coffee, making sure that she saw the clock. Then, if the police asked her later, Jane could say that Thwaite did not leave the house and that Dunn went to catch his train at the right time.

It was a dry night, but very dark. A train carrying freight went slowly by. Thwaite smiled to himself. There were plenty of freight trains at that time of the night. He needed one of them to hide his crime for him. He planned to hit Dunn on the head with the hammer, then put his body on the railway line. A freight train would do the rest.

Slowly, the two men walked on, Thwaite holding Dunn's arm. A light wind moved among the trees. Thwaite gently pushed the half-asleep Dunn forwards. He put his hand into his pocket for the hammer . . .

And stopped.

His keys! They were still inside the house, and he could not get back in without them! He would have to ring the front door bell. His alibi was destroyed!

It was a bad mistake. Everything was wrong now. He couldn't go on with the murder.

'Most murderers make mistakes,' thought Thwaite, trying to calm himself. 'I've been the same.' But he was shaking with fear as he thought about the mistake. Suddenly, he could not walk another step with Dunn.

'Goodnight,' he said to the other man.

And before they reached the crossing, he turned and walked back to the house.

For ten minutes, Thwaite walked up and down outside until he began to feel calm again. Then he rang the bell.

A few moments later, Jane opened the door.

'Thank you, Jane,' he said. 'I went to see Mr Dunn over the crossing, and I forgot my keys.'

He went to bed a happier man. He was not a murderer.

When he was eating his breakfast the next morning, he decided what to do. 'I'll tell them at the office that I stole the thousand pounds,' he said to himself. 'I'll take my punishment, and then I can have some peace again.'

It suddenly seemed so easy.

Until Jane came in.

31

'Have you heard the news, sir?' she said. 'Mr Dunn was killed by a train on the crossing last night. A man who was working on the railway line found him this morning.'

Thwaite slowly went white. Jane was looking at him strangely. What was she thinking? What story did he tell her the night before? He couldn't remember!

'Dunn killed!' he said. 'How terrible, Jane! I'll go down.'

The body was in a small railway building, near the line. There was a policeman outside.

'A sad accident, Mr Thwaite,' the policeman said. 'You knew the man, didn't you, sir?'

'He worked in my office,' replied Thwaite. 'He was with me last night, discussing business. I suppose this happened on his way home. It's terrible!'

'It's very sad, sir,' said the policeman. 'But accidents will happen.'

'I know that,' said Thwaite. 'But I wish he hadn't drunk so much of my whisky. I was going to walk with him to the station.'

The policeman looked closely at Thwaite. 'And did you, sir?'

'No,' said Thwaite. 'The cold night air seemed to make him feel better. I turned back before the crossing.'

The policeman said no more, but later that day two more policemen came to the office. 'Have they talked to Jane?' wondered Thwaite. Again he told them, 'I left Dunn before we reached the railway crossing.' They wrote down what he said to them, then went away.

Next day, they came back.

There were things that Thwaite could not explain to them. Why did the whisky bottle contain what was left of a sleeping powder? Why was the study clock wrong by ten minutes? (At dinner-time earlier on the same evening, Jane had noticed that it was right.) And why was a hammer found in his overcoat pocket?

Then the police found papers in Dunn's house. The handwriting on them was Dunn's. It told the story of Thwaite and the thousand pounds, and it told how Thwaite was a thief. The police then discovered that money taken from Thwaite's bank account over the last five years always appeared a few days later in Dunn's bank book.

Lastly, the time of death was known to be 10.30 pm because Dunn's blood was found on the train that went through the railway crossing at that time. *It was also seven minutes before Jane opened the front door to let Thwaite back in.*

At first, Thwaite had no answers to all their questions.

Finally, on his last morning, he told them the true story. Then he went to his death bravely.

WORD FOCUS

Match each word with an appropriate meaning.

alibi	things (to buy or sell) that are taken by train or ship
blackmail(ing)	a strong drink
freight	a small electric light which is carried in the hand
hammer	to get money from someone by saying you will tell bad things about them
murder	
railway crossing	a tool with a wooden handle and a heavy metal head
	to kill a person
sleeping powder	something to show you were not there when a crime happened
torch	a place where a road and a railway line cross each other
whisky	something taken to help you sleep

Perhaps a policeman made some notes in his notebook while working on the case. Complete his notes with six of the nine words from the list above.

Dunstan Thwaite said that he planned to ___ John Dunn. But he did not do it. Thwaite wanted to kill Dunn because Dunn was ___ him. Thwaite invited Dunn to his home and gave him some ___ to drink. The whisky had a ___ ___ in it. Thwaite changed the time on the clock in his study and on his watch to give himself an ___. But the murder plan went wrong. Thwaite walked with Dunn towards the station, but Thwaite went home before they got to the ___ ___.

STORY FOCUS

Here are three short passages from the story. Read them and answer the questions.

> 'I need a hundred pounds . . . for my son. He's in a bit of trouble, you see . . .'

1 Who says these words, and to whom?
2 Where does this conversation take place?
3 Why does the speaker talk about his son when the other person knows that he does not have one?

> 'Five hundred! . . . Why not ask for the moon?'

4 Who says these words, and to whom?
5 What are they talking about?
6 What do you think the speaker means when he says, 'Why not ask for the moon?'

> 'You can go and do your worst.'

7 Where does this conversation take place?
8 What do you think 'your worst' means here?
9 Is this a dangerous thing for the speaker to say? Why, or why not?

The Daffodil Sky

~

Is it a good idea to re-visit the past, to go back to places you once lived in, to search for people you knew many years before? Places change, people change . . . Who knows what you might learn, and who you might meet?

Under a stormy, daffodil-yellow sky, Bill walks slowly through the streets of his home town. He has come home after eighteen years away. And as he walks, he remembers the past – the daffodils he used to sell, the girl he loved, and the day that destroyed his hopes and his dreams . . .

The Daffodil Sky

Retold by Rosemary Border

Bill got off the train, under a stormy, dark yellow sky. Automatically, he went to the railway footbridge. That was always the quickest way to the town. He could save half a mile that way. And then he saw that the footbridge was closed. There was a big blue notice board. 'Danger. Keep Off.'

'This town has changed,' he said to himself.

So he went the long way, past the factories and along the thin black railway line. Soon he came to a pub. In the old days, Bill often stopped there on his way to market.

In those days he used to come into town every week. He brought his fruit and vegetables or, in early spring, his daffodils, and sold them in the market. In the early days, he had brought them in a horse and cart. But soon he had been ready to buy his first car . . .

The walls of the pub were black with smoke from passing trains. Bill went through the glass door and walked up to the bar.

'I'll have a beer, please,' he said.

Two railwaymen were playing cards in one corner of the bar.

Bill paid for his beer. 'I'm looking for a Miss Whitehead,' he said. 'She used to come in here. She used to live in Wellington Street and work in the shoe factory there.'

'That was a long time ago,' said the barman. 'They built a new shoe factory ten years ago – outside the town.'

'She used to come in here when Jack Shipley had this pub.'

'Jack Shipley?' said the barman. 'He's been dead nine years now.'

One of the railwaymen looked up from his card game.

'Do you mean Cora Whitehead?' he said.

'That's right.'

'She still lives in Wellington Street with her old Dad.'

'Thanks very much,' said Bill.

He finished his drink and went out. The sky above his head was still that bright, unnatural daffodil yellow. Suddenly he remembered his first visit to this pub. He had called in, many years ago, during a storm, to get a drink of water for his horse and some beer for himself. 'How many years ago was it?' he thought. 'But I still remember everything so clearly.'

⌀

His cart had been full of daffodils, he remembered. They were a bright, burning yellow, like the stormy sky now above his head. He was crossing the bridge when he heard thunder. Then the storm came. He did not have time to cover the cart. 'Come on!' he shouted to his horse. He drove to the pub. He found a dry place for his horse and cart. Then he ran through the rain towards the door of the bar.

'Don't knock me over!' said a girl's voice.

'Sorry,' he said.

He had not noticed the colour of the girl's dress. Perhaps it was blue; he was not sure. But he had noticed her large, full, red mouth, also her long, reddish-brown hair and big brown eyes.

He could not open the door because his hands were wet. She started to laugh. It was a strong, friendly laugh, not too loud. A moment later the sun came out. He felt it on his face and neck.

'You're as good as an umbrella on a wet day,' the girl said.

The door opened at last, and they were inside the pub. There was a smell of smoke and beer, sandwiches and warm bodies. But she said, 'There's a smell of flowers in here. Can you smell it too?'

'I've got a cart full of flowers,' he said. 'Daffodils. I've been picking them since six o'clock this morning. I've got the smell of them on my hands.'

He held up his hands for her to smell.

'That's it,' she said. 'What a lovely smell!'

He watched her as she drank her beer. 'She's beautiful,' he thought. He wanted to be early at the market by twelve o'clock. But he stayed in the pub with her until nearly two. Every time he thought about leaving, the thunder crashed and the rain beat against the window again. Then at last the bright daffodil sun came out again.

'I have to go,' he said.

'You'll be all right,' she said. 'You'll sell all your daffodils. You've got a lucky face. People like you are always lucky.'

'How do you know?'

'I bring them luck,' she said. 'I always do.'

And she was right. All that day, and for a long time

afterwards, Bill was lucky. That evening was clear and fine. Customers came to the market. They saw the shining yellow daffodils and they bought them all. 'She was right,' thought Bill. 'She did bring me luck.'

Soon Bill sold his horse and cart and bought a car. At first he did not think he had enough money.

'Listen,' she said. 'Frankie Corbett's got an old car that he wants to get rid of. I'll have a word with Frankie. It'll be cheap – you'll see.'

She was right. Bill bought the car very cheaply.

'You see,' she said. 'I bring you luck.'

That summer Bill began to visit the house in Wellington Street. Cora's mother was dead and her father worked all night on the railway. So it was easy for them to spend the night together. Those were happy times. They did not talk much, but they were very happy. She understood him so well.

'Do you know what?' she said sometimes. 'I know when you turn the corner by the bridge. I feel you near me. I know you're coming, every time.'

∝

Bill rented his land from an old man called Osborne. Osborne had a little farm. He had chickens and a few cows and sheep. Most of the land was covered with old fruit trees. In the spring the daffodils grew thickly at the foot of every tree.

'I'm getting old,' Osborne said one day. 'I'd like to go and live with my sister. I'll sell you my farm, cheap. Pay me a deposit and give me the rest of the money later.'

Suddenly Bill saw all his life in front of him like a bright, beautiful carpet. A farm!

That evening he went for a drive with Cora. They stopped in a field full of summer flowers. The long grass hid them from the road. He lay on his back among the flowers. He looked up at the bright blue sky and talked to Cora about his plans. But Cora was not sure.

'How do you know that this Osborne man is honest?'

'I know Osborne. He's as honest as the day is long.'

'Yes, and some days are longer than others,' she said. 'Don't forget that.'

She looked thoughtfully at him with her big, soft brown eyes.

'How much money have you got?' she asked.

'I've saved a hundred and fifty pounds.'

'So you pay Osborne your hundred and fifty pounds as a deposit, and then what do you get?'

'The land. The farm buildings. The animals. The fruit trees. Everything.'

'I don't know,' she said. She lay there for a long time, and looked up at the August sky. Then she shut her eyes, and turned her face towards his. Softly and lovingly they kissed.

After a long time she opened her eyes again.

'I've been thinking,' she said. 'Can I join you in this business? I've got fifty pounds. How much does he want for his farm?'

'A thousand.'

'And we've got two hundred. Can you borrow any more?'

'I don't know where I can get it from.'

'I can get it,' said Cora. 'I'll ask Frankie Corbett. He's got plenty of money – I'll talk to Frankie and ask him to help us.'

Suddenly he was holding her face in his hands. 'We'll get married,' he said. 'You know what you said – you bring me luck.'

They kissed again.

'I'll never forget this day,' thought Bill. 'I feel lucky – the luckiest man in the world. I've got a car, and a house, and a farm . . . and the woman I love.'

'And it all started,' he said aloud, 'with the daffodils.'

'That's how all important things start,' said Cora. 'With something small like a few daffodils. Kiss me again, Bill.'

Six weeks later, on a rainy October evening, he was killing Frankie Corbett . . .

He thought about Frankie Corbett now, as he walked slowly and heavily up Wellington Street, along the rows of smoke-blackened little houses. The sky above the factory chimneys was still dark and stormy.

A man walked up the street with two thin, long-legged dogs beside him. 'That was how Frankie Corbett came that evening,' he remembered. 'But he only had one dog. I knew who he was, because of the dog.'

'Were you waiting for this man?' they had asked him afterwards, all those years ago. But he had only wanted to talk, he told them. That was all. He knew that Frankie Corbett took his dog for a walk every evening. He knew it was a little white, noisy dog. Cora had told him about it.

Bill had not realized how jealous he was. It was not a hot, quick, sudden kind of jealousy. His jealousy was quiet and slow-burning, but it was very strong and deep. It had begun with little things. It started when Cora began to talk about 'Frankie'. 'Frankie will get the money. No, I can't see you tonight because I have to see Frankie.'

He began to feel unsure about her. 'How long have you known this Frankie?' he asked her.

'Oh, I've known Frankie all my life.'

He was worried now. 'Have you . . . ?' He stopped. She knew what he meant, of course. She always understood him so well.

'Oh, we've had a bit of fun sometimes.'

'But . . . is he . . . more than a friend?'

'Oh, we went out together a few times. But we argued all the time. We were no good for each other. He's nothing to me now. But Frankie will do anything for me.'

Bill did not like that. 'What will she do for him in return?' he wondered.

Cora was angry. 'Look,' she said. 'We want the money, don't we? But I can't ask for hundreds of pounds, just like that. Now can I? Be patient.'

It took a month to get the money. Long before the end of the month, his heart was full of jealousy. He could feel it growing inside him, and slowly burning his heart away. He no longer dreamed of the house, the farm, the fruit trees or the daffodils. Instead he dreamed of Cora in another man's arms.

Then came the news about Cora's baby. He was terribly

afraid that it was Frankie Corbett's child. And that was why he waited for Frankie Corbett that evening.

People passed and saw him waiting there. Then a small white dog came along. It yapped at Bill. He knew it was Frankie Corbett's dog. Then Frankie Corbett came. He was much older than Bill. He was carrying a walking-stick.

Bill stopped him. He was shaking violently. 'I must talk to you!' he said thickly. Black and red lines danced in front of his eyes.

It began to rain. 'I'm getting wet,' said Frankie Corbett. 'I can't stand here in the rain, and talk to you.'

'I want an honest answer. That's all,' said Bill. Just then the dog yapped again, and Frankie Corbett lifted his stick angrily.

Suddenly Bill thought that Frankie Corbett meant to hit him with the stick. A minute later Bill was hitting out with his knife. It was a long, thin knife. Bill used it to cut his vegetables. Frankie Corbett fell down and hit his head on the ground.

Cora was right: it was the little things that were important. The knife, the yapping dog, the people who saw him waiting in the rain. And then, of course, there was his jealousy. At the trial they talked a lot about jealousy.

'How can you describe this man's jealousy?' they asked Cora.

'Black jealousy,' said Cora at once. Bill knew that it was true. She always knew how he felt about things. She loved him truly. But her words had sent Bill to prison for eighteen years . . .

❧

84 Wellington Street. Bill was outside the house now. Above his head the stormy sky was getting darker. He heard the crash of thunder, a long way away. His heart was beating fast, and red and black lines danced in front of his eyes. 'I felt like this when I was waiting for Frankie Corbett,' he thought. 'Will she be there? And if she is there, what can I say to her after all this time?'

He knocked on the door. A light came on inside the house. The door began to open. His heart was beating harder than ever. He waited. A girl stood on the doorstep.

'She hasn't changed,' he said to himself. He remembered the day when they met, the day of the daffodils. 'I loved her then,' he thought, 'and I still love her now.'

'Yes?' she said.

The voice was different. It was quieter and lighter. And then he saw her face, and suddenly he knew . . .

'Are you Cora's daughter?' he asked.

'Yes.'

'I'm an old friend of hers . . . When will she come back?'

'Not until late tonight. She's working at the shoe factory.'

'I see,' he said heavily.

Suddenly the thunder crashed and the rain began to fall.

'Come in,' she said. 'Come in and wait until the rain stops.'

'No, I'll get a bus to the station,' he said.

But the rain was coming down like a waterfall.

'You can't go out in this,' she said. 'Stand here in the doorway.'

His heart was beating violently. The blood seemed to

sing in his ears. Her eyes were brown and soft and kind, just like Cora's.

She said, 'Do you have to catch a train? If you don't, perhaps I can lend you an umbrella. You can bring it back tomorrow.'

He looked at the sky above the factory chimneys. 'It looks brighter over there,' he said.

'Wait one more minute,' the girl said. 'Then if the rain doesn't stop, I'll go and get that umbrella.'

He waited, and watched her face. 'Are you still at school?' he asked.

'Oh no! Not me. I work at the shoe factory too. But I work in the daytime.'

Suddenly he was afraid to say any more. 'She's going to ask my name,' he thought, but he was afraid to tell her.

'I must go,' he said. 'I don't want to keep you standing here.'

'I'll get the umbrella,' she said.

Suddenly he remembered her mother's words: 'You're as good as an umbrella on a rainy day.'

Then the girl said, 'I'll walk as far as the bridge with you. It isn't raining very hard now. You can get a bus there and I can bring the umbrella back.'

'I don't want to trouble you . . .'

'Oh! That's all right.' She laughed. Her laugh, too, was like her mother's.

She ran out, and held the umbrella over them both. By accident he touched her arm, and felt almost sick with excitement.

'Why are you hurrying?' she asked suddenly. 'Are you going anywhere special?'

She was right. He was hurrying. The excitement of her nearness was driving him on, through the rain. He laughed.

'Nowhere special,' he said.

'I knew it all the time.'

That was like her mother too. He remembered Cora's words: 'I know when you're coming . . . I feel you near me.'

The rain stopped before they reached the bridge. The sky looked newly washed after the storm. They stood together under that daffodil sky.

'I like being with you,' she said. 'Do you feel like that about some people? You know immediately when you meet them.'

'That's right,' he said.

Suddenly, he wanted to tell her who he was. He wanted to tell her all about himself. He wanted to tell her about her mother, and his lost dream. But he was afraid.

'I can't stay here,' he thought. 'I ought to get out now. I ought to find a little farm like Osborne's, and work there and save my money. I ought to start all over again. There's plenty of farm work at this time of year.'

Then he felt a sudden, awful loneliness. He felt sick and miserable and terribly afraid. He looked up at the yellow sky.

'Will you . . .' he began.

A train went under the bridge with a noise like thunder, and his words were lost. When it had gone, she said, 'What did you say?'

'It doesn't matter. I was just wondering . . . Perhaps you'd like to have a drink with me?'

She smiled. 'Well, what are we waiting for then?'

'Nothing,' said Bill.

They walked together towards the pub. She shook the umbrella and closed it. She looked up at the calm, rain-washed daffodil sky.

'The storm's over,' she said. 'It'll be a lovely day tomorrow.' She smiled again, and he knew she was right.

WORD FOCUS

Perhaps Cora's daughter told her mother about the man who came to the house. When Cora realized that the man was Bill, she told her daughter the story. Use these words to complete what she said (one word in each gap).

beer, cart, daffodils, deposit, jealousy, marry, rented, thunder

'Well, I remember the day I met Bill. It was a stormy day with heavy rain and _____. Bill stopped at the pub to get some water for his horse and some _____ for himself. When he came into the pub, I smelled flowers. He said he had the smell of _____ on his hands because he had picked them to take to the market that morning. I saw his _____ outside, full of lovely, bright, burning yellow flowers. We soon became good friends.

Bill sold vegetables and flowers at the market, and he _____ his land from an old man called Osborne. One day Osborne offered to sell his farm to Bill. Bill had to pay a _____ and give Osborne the rest of the money later. So I decided to help Bill buy the farm – and to _____ him! I knew an older man called Frankie Corbett, who had plenty of money, and my plan was to ask Frankie to help us buy the farm. A month later I got the money from Frankie, but by then Bill had changed . . . his heart was full of black _____ . . .'

STORY FOCUS 1

After Bill's visit to the house, Cora wrote her diary for that day. Here are some sentences from it. Choose an adjective from the list for the first gap, and then write as much as you like to finish the sentences.

afraid, angry, anxious, excited, frightened, happy, jealous, lucky, sad, unhappy

- When I heard that Bill came to the house today, I felt _____ because _____.

- Eighteen years ago, on that spring day when I first met Bill at the pub, I felt _____ because _____.
- I wanted to live on the farm with Bill, so I tried to get some money to help him. But Bill was so _____ when _____.
- It was late evening when the police came to tell me that Bill had killed Frankie Corbett. I was _____ because _____.
- At the end of Bill's trial, I was _____ when _____.

STORY FOCUS 2

1

2

3

4

5

6

Imagine that you are a reporter. After Bill killed Frankie Corbett, you can ask Cora six questions to find out what happened, and why. Which six questions will you ask her?

A Moment
of
Madness

~

Some people find it hard to make decisions. They
wait for things to happen in their lives, and if there
is a problem, they just close their eyes and hope it
will go away. And deciding who to marry can be the
hardest thing of all.

Baptista thinks she has made her decision about
marriage, and is on her way back to her island
home to do what her parents want. But she misses
the boat and has to wait three days until the next
one. In three days, there is more than enough time
for a moment of madness – a moment that will
change her life in some quite unexpected ways . . .

THOMAS HARDY

A Moment of Madness

Retold by Clare West

1
A wedding is arranged

Most people who knew Baptista Trewthen agreed that there was nothing in her to love, and nothing in her to hate. She did not seem to feel very strongly about anything. But still waters run deep, and nothing had yet happened to make her show what lay hidden inside her, like gold underground.

Since her birth she had lived on St Maria's, an island off the south-west coast of England. Her father, a farmer, had spent a lot of money on sending her to school on the mainland. At nineteen she studied at a training college for teachers, and at twenty-one she found a teaching job in a town called Tor-upon-Sea, on the mainland coast.

Baptista taught the children as well as she could, but after a year had passed she seemed worried about something. Mrs Wace, her landlady, noticed the change in the young woman and asked her what the matter was.

'It has nothing to do with the town, or you,' replied Miss Trewthen. She seemed reluctant to say more.

'Then is it the pay?'

'No, it isn't the pay.'

'Is it something that you've heard from home, my dear?'

Baptista was silent for a few moments. Then she said, 'It's Mr Heddegan – David Heddegan. He's an old neighbour of ours on St Maria's, with no wife or family at all. When I was a child, he used to say he wanted to marry me one day. Now I'm a woman, it's no longer a joke, and he really wishes to do it. And my parents say I can't do better than have him.'

'Has he a lot of money?'

'Yes, he's the richest man that we know.'

'How much older than you is he?'

'Twenty years, maybe more.'

'And is he, perhaps, an unpleasant man?'

'No, he's not unpleasant.'

'Well, child, all I can say is this – don't accept this engagement if it doesn't please you. You're comfortable here in my house, I hope, and I like having you here.'

'Thank you, Mrs Wace. You're very kind to me. But here comes my difficulty. I don't like teaching. Ah, you're surprised. That's because I've hidden it from everyone. Well, I really hate school. The children are awful little things, who make trouble all day long. But even *they* are not as bad as the inspector. For the three months before his visit I woke up several times every night, worrying about it. It's so difficult knowing what to teach and what to leave untaught! I think father and mother are right. They say I'll never be a good teacher if I don't like the work, so I should marry Mr Heddegan and then I won't need to work. I don't know what to do, Mrs Wace. I like him better than teaching, but I don't like him enough to marry him.'

These conversations were continued from day to day, until at last the landlady decided to agree with Baptista's parents.

'Life will be much easier for you, my dear,' she told her young friend, 'if you marry this rich neighbour.'

In April Baptista went home to St Maria's for a short holiday, and when she returned, she seemed calmer.

'I have agreed to have him as my husband, so that's the end of it,' she told Mrs Wace.

In the next few months letters passed between Baptista and Mr Heddegan, but the girl preferred not to discuss her engagement with Mrs Wace. Later, she told her that she was leaving her job at the end of July, and the wedding was arranged for the first Wednesday in August.

2
A chance meeting

When the end of July arrived, Baptista was in no hurry to return home to the island. She was not planning to buy any special clothes for the wedding, and her parents were making all the other arrangements. So she did not leave Tor-upon-Sea until the Saturday before her wedding. She travelled by train to the town of Pen-zephyr, but when she arrived, she found that the boat to St Maria's had left early, and there was no other boat until Tuesday. 'I'll have to stay here until then,' she thought. 'It's too far to go back to Mrs Wace's.' She did not seem to mind this – in fact, she was almost happy to wait another three nights before seeing her future husband.

She found a room in a small hotel, took her luggage there, then went out for a walk round the town.

'Baptista? Yes, Baptista it is!'

The words came from behind her. Turning round, she gave a jump, and stared. 'Oh, is it really you, Charles?' she said.

With a half-smile the newcomer looked her up and down. He appeared almost angry with her, but he said nothing.

'I'm going home,' she continued, 'but I've missed the boat.'

He did not seem interested in this news. 'Still teaching?' he said. 'What a fine teacher you make, Baptista, I'm sure!'

She knew that was not his real meaning. 'I know I'm not very good at teaching,' she replied. 'That's why I've stopped.'

'Oh, you've stopped? You surprise me.'

'I hate teaching.'

'Perhaps that's because *I'm* a teacher.'

'Oh no, it isn't. It's because I'm starting a new life. Next week I'm going to marry Mr David Heddegan.'

At this unexpected reply, the young man took a step back. 'Who is Mr David Heddegan?' he said, trying to sound bored.

'He owns a number of shops on St Maria's, and he's my father's neighbour and oldest friend.'

'So, no longer a schoolteacher, just a shopkeeper's wife. I knew you would never succeed as a teacher. You're like a woman who thinks she can be a great actress just because she has a beautiful face, and forgets she has to be able to act. But you found out your mistake early, didn't you?'

'Don't be unpleasant to me, Charles,' Baptista said sadly.

'I'm not being unpleasant – I'm just saying what is true, in a friendly way – although I do have good reason to be unpleasant to you. What a hurry you've been in, Baptista! I do hate a woman in a hurry!'

'What do you mean?'

'Well – in a hurry to be somebody's wife. Any husband is better than no husband for you, it seems. You couldn't wait for me, oh no! Well, thank God, that's all in the past for me!'

'Wait for you? What does that mean, Charley? You never showed that you felt anything special for me.'

'Oh really, Baptista dear!'

'What I mean is, there was nothing that I could be sure of. I suppose you liked me a little, but I didn't think you meant to make an honest engagement of it.'

'That's just it! You girls expect a man to talk about marrying after the first look! But I *did* mean to get engaged to you, you know.'

'But you never said so, and a woman can't wait for ever!'

'Baptista, I promise you that I was planning to ask you to marry me in six months' time.'

She appeared very uncomfortable, and they walked

along in silence. Soon he said, 'Did you want to marry me then?'

And she whispered sadly back, 'Yes!'

As they walked on, away from the town and into the fields, her shoulder and his were close together. He held her arm with a strong hand. This seemed to say, 'Now I hold you, and you must do what I want.'

'How strange that we should meet like this!' said the young man. 'You and I could be husband and wife, going on our honeymoon together. But instead of that, we'll say goodbye in half an hour, perhaps for ever. Yes, life is strange!'

She stopped walking. 'I must go back. This is too painful, Charley! You're not being kind today.'

'I don't want to hurt you – you know I don't,' he answered more gently. 'But it makes me angry – what you're going to do. I don't think you should marry him.'

'I must do it, now that I've agreed.'

'Why?' he asked, speaking more seriously now. 'It's never too late to stop a wedding if you're not happy with it. Now – you could marry me, instead of him, although you were in too much of a hurry to wait for me!'

'Oh, it isn't possible to think of that!' she cried, shaking her head. 'At home everything will be ready for the wedding!'

'If we marry, it must be at once. This evening you can come back with me to Trufal, the town where I live. We can get married there on Tuesday, and then no Mr David Heddegan, or anyone else, can take you away from me!'

'But I must go home on the Tuesday boat,' she said worriedly. 'What will they think if I don't arrive?'

'You can go home on that boat just the same. The only difference is that I'll go with you. You'll tell your parents that you've married a young man with a good job, someone that you met at the training college. When I meet them, they'll accept that we're married and it can't be changed. And you won't be miserable for ever as the wife of an awful old man. Now honestly, you do like me best, don't you, Baptista?'

'Yes,' she whispered.

'Then we will do what I say.'

3
Baptista gets married

That same afternoon Charles Stow and Baptista Trewthen travelled by train to the town of Trufal. Charles was, surprisingly, very careful of appearances, and found a room for Baptista in a different house from where he was staying. On Sunday they went to church and then walked around the town, on Monday Charles made the arrangements, and by nine o'clock on Tuesday morning they were husband and wife.

For the first time in her life Baptista had gone against her parents' wishes. She went cold with fear when she thought of their first meeting with her new husband. But she felt she had to tell them as soon as possible, and now the most important thing was to get home to St Maria's. So, in a great hurry, they packed their bags and caught the train to Pen-zephyr.

They arrived two hours before the boat left, so to pass the time they decided to walk along the cliffs a little way. It was a hot summer day, and Charles wanted to have a swim in the sea. Baptista did not like the idea of sitting alone while he swam. 'But I'll only be a quarter of an hour,' Charles said, and Baptista passively accepted this.

She sat high up on the cliffs, and watched him go down a footpath, disappear, appear again, and run across the beach to the sea. She watched him for a moment, then stared out to sea, thinking about her family. They were probably not worried about her, because she had sometimes missed the boat before, but they were expecting her to arrive today – and to marry David Heddegan tomorrow. 'How angry father will be!' she thought miserably. 'And mother will say I've made a terrible mistake! I almost wish I hadn't married Charles, in that moment of madness! Oh dear, what have I done!'

This made her think of her new husband, and she turned to look for him. He did not appear to be in the sea any more, and she could not see him on the beach. By this time she was frightened, and she climbed down the path as quickly as her shaking legs could manage. On the beach she called two men to help her, but they said they could see nothing at all in the water. Soon she found the place where Charles had left his clothes, but by now the sea had carried them away.

For a few minutes she stood there without moving. There was only one way to explain this sudden disappearance – her husband had drowned. And as she stood there, it began to seem like a terrible dream, and the last three days of her life with Charles seemed to disappear. She even had difficulty in remembering his face. 'How unexpected it was, meeting him that day!' she thought. 'And the wedding – did I really agree to it? Are we really married? It all happened so fast!'

She began to cry, still standing there on the beach. She did not know what to do, or even what to think. Finally, she remembered the boat, and catching the boat home seemed the easiest thing to do. So she walked to the station, arranged for someone to carry her luggage, and went down to the boat. She did all this automatically, in a kind of dream.

Just before the boat left, she heard part of a conversation which made her sure that Charles was dead. One passenger said to another, 'A man drowned here earlier today, you know. He swam out too far, they say. A stranger, I think. Some people in a boat saw him, but they couldn't get to him in time.'

The boat was a long way out to sea before Baptista realized that Mr Heddegan was on the boat with her. She saw him walking towards her and quickly took the wedding ring off her left hand.

'I hope you're well, my dear?' he said. He was a healthy, red-faced man of fifty-five. 'I wanted to come across to meet you. What bad luck that you missed the boat on Saturday!'

And Baptista had to agree, and smile, and make conversation. Mr Heddegan had spoken to her before she was ready to say anything. Now the moment had passed.

When the boat arrived, her parents were there to meet her. Her father walked home beside Mr Heddegan, while her mother walked next to Baptista, talking all the time.

'I'm so happy, my child,' said Mrs Trewthen in her loud, cheerful voice, 'that you've kept your promise to marry Mr Heddegan. How busy we've been! But now things are all ready for the wedding, and a few friends and neighbours are coming in for supper this evening.' Again, the moment for confessing had passed, and Baptista stayed silent.

When they reached home, Mrs Trewthen said, 'Now, Baptista, hurry up to your room and take off your hat, then come downstairs. I must go to the kitchen.'

The young woman passively obeyed her mother's orders. The evening was a great success for all except Baptista. She had no chance to tell her parents the news, and it was already much more difficult than it had been at first. By the end of the evening, when all the neighbours had left, she found herself alone in her bedroom again. She had come home with much to say, and had said none of it. She now realized that she was not brave enough to tell her story. And as the clock struck midnight, she decided it should stay untold.

Morning came, and when she thought of Charles, it was

more with fear than with love. Her mother called from downstairs, 'Baptista! Time to get up! Mr Heddegan will be at the church in three-quarters of an hour!'

Baptista got out of bed, looked out of the window, and took the easy way. She put her best clothes on, confessed nothing, and kept her promise to marry David Heddegan.

4

The honeymoon

Mr Heddegan did not worry about his new wife's coldness towards him during and after the wedding. 'I know she was reluctant to marry me,' he thought, 'but that will pass. Things'll be different in a few months' time!'

During the wedding dinner, someone asked Heddegan about the honeymoon. To Baptista's horror, he answered, 'Oh, we're going to spend a few days in Pen-zephyr.'

'What!' cried Baptista. 'I know nothing of this!'

Because of her late arrival, Heddegan had not been able to ask where *she* would like to spend the honeymoon, so he had arranged a trip to the mainland. It was difficult to change these plans at the last minute, so she had to agree, and that evening she and her new husband arrived in Pen-zephyr.

Their first problem was finding a hotel, because the fine weather had filled the town with tourists. They walked from place to place, Heddegan polite and friendly, Baptista cold and silent. Finally they found an excellent hotel, which to their surprise was empty. Kindly Mr Heddegan, who wanted to please his young wife, asked for the best room on the first floor, with a good view of the sea.

'I'm sorry,' said the landlady, 'there's a gentleman in that room.' Then, seeing Heddegan's disappointed face, and not wishing to lose a customer, she added quickly, 'But perhaps the gentleman will agree to move to another room, and then you can have the one that you want.'

'Well, if he doesn't want a view . . .' said Mr Heddegan.

'Oh no, I'm sure he doesn't. And if you don't mind going for a little walk, I'll have the room ready when you return.'

During their walk, Baptista was careful to choose different streets from those that she had walked down with Charles, and her white face showed how difficult this visit was for her. At last they returned to the hotel, and were shown into the best bedroom. They sat at the window, drinking tea. Although Heddegan had arranged for a sea view, to please Baptista, she did not look out of the window once, but kept her eyes on the floor and walls of the room.

Suddenly she noticed a hat on the back of the door. It was just like the hat that Charles had worn. She stared harder; yes, it was the actual hat! She fell back in her chair.

Her husband jumped up, saying worriedly, 'You're not well! What can I get ye?'

'Smelling salts!' she said quickly, her voice shaking a little. 'From the shop near the station!'

He ran out of the room. Baptista rang the bell, and when a young girl came, whispered to her, 'That hat! Whose is it?'

'Oh, I'm sorry, I'll take it away,' said the girl hurriedly. She took the hat off the door. 'It belongs to the other gentleman.'

'Where is – the other gentleman?' asked Baptista.

'He's in the next room, madam. He *was* in here.'

'But I can't hear him! I don't think he's there.'

'He makes no noise, but he's there,' replied the girl.

Suddenly Baptista understood what the girl meant, and a cold hand lay on her heart.

'Why is he so silent?' she whispered.

'If I tell you, please don't say anything to the landlady,' begged the girl, 'or I'll lose my job! It's because he's dead. He's the young teacher who drowned yesterday. They brought his body here, and that's why there's nobody staying in the hotel. People don't like a dead body in the house. But we've changed the sheets and cleaned the room, madam!'

Just then Heddegan arrived with the smelling salts, and the girl left the room. 'Any better?' he asked Baptista.

'I don't like the hotel!' she cried. 'We'll have to leave!'

For the first time Heddegan spoke crossly to his wife. 'Now that's enough, Baptista! First you want one thing, then another! It's cost me enough, in money and words, to get this fine room, and it's too much to expect me to find another hotel at this time of the evening. We'll stay quietly here tonight, do ye hear? And find another place tomorrow.'

The young woman said no more. Her mind was cold with horror. That night she lay between the two men who she had married, David Heddegan on one side, and, on the other side through the bedroom wall, Charles Stow.

5
Secrets discovered

Mr and Mrs Heddegan both felt the honeymoon was not a success. They were happy to return to the island and start married life together in David Heddegan's large house. Baptista soon became as calm and passive as she had been before. She even smiled when neighbours called her Mrs Heddegan, and she began to enjoy the comfortable life that a rich husband could offer her. She did nothing at all to stop people finding out about her first marriage to Charles Stow, although there was always a danger of that happening.

One evening in September, when she was standing in her garden, a workman walked past along the road. He seemed to recognize her, and spoke to her in friendly surprise.

'What! Don't you know me?' he asked.

'I'm afraid I don't,' said Baptista.

'I was your witness, madam. I was mending the church window when you and your young man came to get married. Don't you remember? The vicar called me, to be a witness.'

Baptista looked quickly around. Heddegan was at the other end of the garden but unluckily, just at that moment, he turned and walked towards the house. 'Are you coming in, my dear?' he called out to Baptista.

The workman stared at him. 'That's not your—' he began, then he saw Baptista's face and stopped. Baptista was unable to speak, and the workman began to realize that there was a little mystery here. 'I've been unlucky since then,' he continued, still staring at Baptista's white face. 'It's hard finding enough work to buy food for my wife and myself. Perhaps you could help me, because I once helped you?'

Baptista gave him some money, and hoped never to see him again. But he was cleverer than he looked. By asking questions on the island and the mainland, he soon realized that Baptista had married one man on Tuesday, and another man on Wednesday. He visited her again two days later.

'It was a mystery to me, madam!' he said, when she opened the door. 'But now I understand it all. I want to tell you, madam, that I'm not a man to make trouble between husband and wife. But I'm going back to the mainland again, and I need a little more money. If your old man finds out about your first husband, I'm sure he won't like it, will he?'

She knew he was right, and paid him what he wanted. A week later the workman sent his wife to ask for more money, and again Baptista paid. But when there was a fourth visit, she refused to pay, and shut the door in the man's surprised face.

She knew she had to tell her husband everything. She liked him better now than she had done at first, and did not want to lose him, but her secret was no longer safe. She

68

went to find him, and said, 'David, I have something to tell you.'

'Yes, my dear,' he said with a sigh. In the last week he had been less cheerful and had seemed worried about something.

When they were both in the sitting room, she said, 'David, perhaps you will hate me for this, but I must confess something that I've hidden from you. It happened before we were married. And it's about a lover.'

'I don't mind. In fact, I was hoping it was more than that.'

'Well, it was. I met my old lover by chance, and he asked me, and – well, I married him. We were coming here to tell you, but he drowned, and I said nothing about him, and then I married you, David, for peace and quietness. Now you'll be angry with me, I know you will!'

She spoke wildly, and expected her husband to shout and scream. But instead, the old man jumped up and began to dance happily around the room.

'Oh, wonderful!' he cried. 'How lucky! My dear Baptista, I see a way out of my difficulty – ha-ha!'

'What do you mean?' she asked, afraid he had gone mad.

'Oh my dear, *I've* got something to confess too! You see, I was friendly with a woman in Pen-zephyr for many years – *very* friendly, you could say – and in the end I married her just before she died. I kept it secret, but people here are beginning to talk. And I've got four big girls to think of—'

'Oh David, four daughters!' she cried in horror.

'That's right, my dear. I'm sorry to say they haven't been

to school at all. I'd like to bring them to live here with us, and I thought, by marrying a teacher, I could get someone to teach them, all for nothing. What do you think, Baptista?'

'Four grown girls, always around the house! And I hate teaching, it kills me! But I must do it, I can see that. I am punished for that moment of madness, I really am!'

Here the conversation ended. The next day Baptista had to welcome her husband's daughters into her home. They were not good-looking or intelligent or even well-dressed, and poor Baptista could only look forward to years of hard work with them. She went about, sighing miserably, with no hope for the future.

But when Heddegan asked her a month later, 'How do you like 'em now?' her answer was unexpected.

'Much better than at first,' she said. 'I may like them very much one day.'

And so began a more pleasant time for Baptista Heddegan. She had discovered what kind, gentle girls these unwelcome daughters were. At first she felt sorry for them, then grew to like them. And from liking, she grew to love them. In the end they brought her and her husband closer together, and so Baptista and David were able to put the past behind them and find unexpected happiness in their married life.

WORD FOCUS

Choose words from the list to complete these sentences (one word for each gap). There are thirteen words in the list, but only ten of them will be needed.

arranged, cliffs, confess, drown, engagement, honeymoon, horror, landlady, madness, mainland, passive, reluctant, witness

1 After studying at the teacher's college, Baptista found a job in a town called Tor-upon-Sea, which is on the _____ coast.
2 Mrs Wace owned the house where Baptista lived, so Mrs Wace was her _____.
3 Baptista sat high up on the _____ when Charles went to swim in the sea.
4 While her new husband was swimming, Baptista was beginning to wish that she hadn't married him, in that moment of _____.
5 During the wedding dinner, Baptista learnt that Mr Heddegan was going to take her to Pen-zephyr for their _____.
6 Baptista became calm and _____ when she returned to the island and started married life with Mr Heddegan.
7 Mr Heddegan was not worried about his new wife's coldness towards him because he knew that Baptista had been _____ to marry him.
8 The workman who asked Baptista for money was the _____ at the wedding when Baptista married Charles Stow.
9 When Baptista told Mr Heddegan her secret, he was very happy and told her that he had something to _____ too.
10 Mr Heddegan had four grown daughters, and when Baptista heard this unwelcome news, she cried out in _____.

71

Story Focus 1

What do you think about the people in this story? Did Baptista behave sensibly? Choose names from the story and complete these sentences, using as many words as you like.

Baptista, David Heddegan, Mrs Wace, Charles Stow, the workman

1 I think _____ did a very bad thing when _____.
2 I think _____ was right to _____.
3 I think _____ was wrong to _____.
4 I don't think it was very sensible of _____ to _____.
5 I don't think it was very kind of _____ to _____.

Story Focus 2

Match these halves of sentences to make a paragraph of five sentences. Who do you think the narrator is here?

1 One day, when I was mending a church window, . . .
2 A young schoolteacher and a young woman got married, . . .
3 Later, I moved to the island to find work, but I was unlucky, . . .
4 I walked past a house one day and saw the young woman in her garden, . . .
5 I told the woman that I knew her secret, . . .

6 . . . because it was hard to find enough work to buy food for myself and my wife.
7 . . . so she gave me money three times to keep me quiet.
8 . . . the vicar called me to be a witness at a wedding.
9 . . . but they didn't have any family or friends at their wedding.
10 . . . but her husband was not the man that I saw her marry!

The Secret

~

Reporters look for news, and send back their
reports on everything from weddings to wars, from
crime to discoveries in science. And good reporters
dig deep – they dig to find the truth behind the
stories, the real truth, and they don't take no for an
answer.

Henry Cooper is a responsible reporter, who
sends back accurate reports. When he goes to the
new city built on the Moon, he expects to send the
usual Moon news back to Earth. But this time he
thinks people are hiding a news story from him,
and he starts to dig . . .

ARTHUR C. CLARKE

The Secret

Retold by Jennifer Bassett

Henry Cooper had been on the Moon for almost two weeks before he discovered that something was wrong. At first he just had a kind of strange feeling that he couldn't explain, but he was a sensible science reporter so he didn't worry about it too much.

The reason he was here, after all, was because the United Nations Space Administration had asked him to come. UNSA always liked to get sensible, responsible people to send the Moon news back to Earth. It was even more important these days, when an overcrowded world was screaming for more roads and schools and sea farms, and getting angry about all the money that was spent on space research.

So here he was, on his second visit to the Moon, and sending back reports of two thousand words a day. The Moon no longer felt strange to him, but there remained the mystery and wonder of a world as big as Africa, and still almost completely unknown. Just a stone's throw away from the enclosed Plato City was a great, silent emptiness that would test human cleverness for centuries to come.

Cooper had already visited and written about the famous place where the first men had landed on the Moon. But that now belonged to the past, like Columbus's voyage to

America, and the Wright brothers, who built and flew successfully the first plane with an engine. What interested Cooper now was the future.

When he had landed at Archimedes Spaceport, everyone had been very glad to see him. Everything was arranged for his tour, and he could go where he liked, ask any questions he wanted. UNSA had always been friendly towards him because the reports and stories he sent back to Earth were accurate.

But something was wrong somewhere, and he was going to find out what it was.

He reached for the phone and said, 'Please get me the Police Office. I want to speak to the Chief Inspector.'

∝

He met Chandra Coomaraswamy next day in the little park that Plato City was so proud of. It was early in the morning (by clock time, that is, as one Moon day was as long as twenty-eight Earth days), and there was no one around. Cooper had known the Police Chief for many years and for a while they talked about old friends and old times.

Then Cooper said, 'You know everything that's happening on the Moon, Chandra. And you know that I'm here to do a number of reports for UNSA. So why are people trying to hide things from me?'

It was impossible to hurry Chandra. He just went on smoking his pipe until he was ready to answer.

'What people?' he asked at last.

'You really don't know?'

The Chief Inspector shook his head. 'Not an idea,' he said;

and Cooper knew that he was telling the truth. Chandra might be silent, but he would not lie.

'Well, the main thing that I've noticed – and it frightens me a lot – is that the Medical Research Group is avoiding me. Last time I was here, everyone was very friendly, and gave me some fine stories. But now, I can't even meet the research boss. He's always too busy, or on the other side of the Moon. What kind of man is he?'

'Dr Hastings? A difficult man. Very clever, but not easy to work with.'

'What could he be trying to hide?'

'Oh, I'm just a simple policeman. But I'm sure a news reporter like you has some interesting ideas about it.'

'Well,' said Cooper, 'it can't be anything criminal – not in these times. So that leaves one big worry, which really frightens me. Some kind of new, killer disease. Suppose that a spaceship has come back from Mars or somewhere, carrying some really terrible disease – and the doctors can't do anything about it?'

There was a long silence. Then Chandra said, 'I'll start asking some questions. *I* don't like it either, because here's something that you probably don't know. There were three nervous breakdowns in the Medical Group last month – and that's very, very unusual.'

∽

The call came two weeks later, in the middle of the night – the real Moon night. By Plato City time, it was Sunday morning.

'Henry? Chandra here. Can you meet me in half an hour at Airlock Five? Good. I'll see you there.'

This was it, Cooper knew. Airlock Five meant that they were going outside the city. Chandra had found something.

As the Moon car drove along the rough road from the city, Cooper could see the Earth, low in the southern sky. It was almost full, and threw a bright blue-green light over the hard, ugly land of the Moon. It was difficult, Cooper told himself, to see how the Moon could ever be a welcoming place. But if humans wanted to know nature's secrets, it was to places like these that they must come.

The car turned off on to another road and in a while came to a shining glass building standing alone. There was another Moon car, with a red cross on its side, parked by the entrance. Soon they had passed through the airlock, and Cooper was following Chandra down a long hall, past laboratories and computer rooms, all empty on this Sunday morning. At last they came into a large round room in the centre of the building, which was filled with all kinds of plants and small animals from Earth. Waiting there, was a short, grey-haired man, looking very worried, and very unhappy.

'Dr Hastings,' said Coomaraswamy, 'meet Mr Cooper.' He turned to Cooper and added, 'I've persuaded the doctor that there's only one way to keep you quiet – and that's to tell you everything.'

The scientist was not interested in shaking hands or making polite conversation. He walked over to one of the containers, took out a small brown animal, and held it out towards Cooper.

'Do you know what this is?' he asked, unsmiling.

'Of course,' said Cooper. 'A hamster – used in laboratories everywhere.'

'Yes,' said Hastings. 'A perfectly normal golden hamster. Except that this one is five years old – like all the others in this container.'

'Well? What's strange about that?'

'Oh, nothing, nothing at all . . . except for the unimportant fact that hamsters live for only two years. And we have some here that are nearly ten years old.'

For a moment no one spoke, but the room was not silent. It was full of the sounds of the movements and cries of small animals. Then Cooper whispered, 'My God – you've found a way to make life longer!'

'Oh no,' Hastings said. 'We've not found it. The Moon has given it to us . . . and the reason has been right under our noses all the time.' He seemed calmer now, and more in control of himself. 'On Earth,' he went on, 'we spend our whole lives fighting gravity. Every step we take, every movement we make, is hard work for our bodies. In seventy years, how much blood does the heart lift through how many kilometres? But here on the Moon, where an eighty-kilo human weighs only about thirteen kilos, a body has to do only a sixth of that work.'

'I see,' said Cooper slowly. 'Ten years for a hamster – and how long for a human?'

'It's not a simple scientific law,' answered Hastings. 'It depends on a number of things, and a month ago we really didn't know. But now we're quite certain: on the Moon, a human life will last at least two hundred years.'

'And you've been trying to keep it secret!'

'You fool! Don't you understand?'

'Take it easy, Doctor – take it easy,' said Chandra softly.

Hastings took a deep breath and got himself under control again. He began to speak with icy calmness, and his words fell like freezing raindrops into Cooper's mind.

'Think of them up there,' he said, waving his hand upwards to the unseen Earth. 'Six billion of them, packed on to land which isn't big enough to hold them all. Already they're crowding over into the sea beds. And here, there are only a hundred thousand of us, on an almost empty world. But a world where we need years and years of scientific and engineering work just to make life possible; a world where only a few of the brightest and most intelligent scientists can get a job.

'And now we find that we can live for two hundred years. Imagine how they're going to feel about *that* news! This is your problem now, Mr Newsman; you've asked for it, and you've got it. Tell me this, please – I'd really be interested to know – *just how are you going to tell them?*'

He waited, and waited. Cooper opened his mouth, then closed it again, unable to think of anything to say.

In the far corner of the room, one of the baby animals began to cry.

WORD FOCUS

Match each word with an appropriate meaning.

gravity   detailed study in order to discover new facts or information

hamster   the sky and everything beyond it, to the last star

laboratory   the study of all natural things (e.g. physics, biology)

nervous   a small animal like a rat or mouse

research   a room or building used for scientific research

science   the force that on earth pulls things towards the centre of the planet, so that things fall to the ground when dropped

scientist   worried and afraid

space   somebody who works with or studies one of the sciences

After his meeting with Dr Hastings, perhaps Henry Cooper began to write his report for Earth. Complete his report with five of the eight words from the list above.

The Medical _____ Group here on the Moon was avoiding me, so I asked the Chief Inspector to help me. The Chief Inspector took me to a _____ where I met Dr Hastings. Dr Hastings is a _____ who studies medical problems. When I met Dr Hastings, he showed me a small _____, which he said was five years old. He then told me that on Earth a hamster lives for only two years, but some hamsters on the Moon were nearly ten years old. The reason, Dr Hastings explained, is that on Earth a body spends its whole life fighting _____, but on the Moon a body has to do only one sixth of that work. So on the Moon a human life could last for more than two hundred years . . .

STORY FOCUS 1

Here are four new endings for the story. Which do you prefer? Explain why or write a new ending for yourself.

1 Henry Cooper sent a report to Earth. When people heard that humans could live for more than two hundred years on the Moon, there were many problems. Countries soon began to fight each other so that they could send their people to the Moon . . .

2 After Henry Cooper had thought about the secret for a while, he told Dr Hastings and the Chief Inspector that he would not send a report to Earth *if* he himself was allowed to live on the Moon . . .

3 Henry Cooper left the laboratory in the Moon car, but he never returned to Plato City. And he was never seen again . . .

4 After Henry Cooper spoke to Dr Hastings, he sent a news report to Earth. But he wrote about something else; he kept the secret to himself for the rest of his life . . .

STORY FOCUS 2

Later, perhaps Henry thought about the secret and made a chart to help himself decide what to do. Fill in the chart giving at least two reasons for each side.

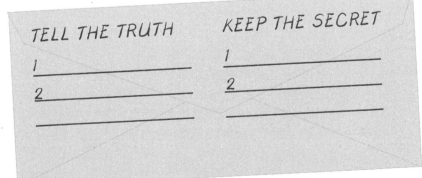

TELL THE TRUTH

1 _____

2 _____

_____

KEEP THE SECRET

1 _____

2 _____

_____

The Experiment

~

Years ago, people used to believe many strange things. They believed that the dead do not always lie quietly in their graves. Sometimes they have unfinished business with the world, and they come back to bring trouble and fear to the living.

Squire Bowles has some strange ideas about what happens to a man's soul after death. And when he is taken ill and dies suddenly, he certainly leaves unfinished business behind him. His wife and stepson have a question to ask, but only the Squire knows the answer, and how can you ask a question of a man who lies dead in his grave?

The Experiment

Retold by Peter Hawkins

In the last days of December, Dr Hall, the village priest, was working in his study when his servant entered the room, in great alarm.

'Oh, Dr Hall, sir,' she cried. 'What do you think? The poor Squire's dead!'

'What? Squire Bowles? What are you saying, woman?' replied the priest. 'I saw him only yesterday—'

'Yes, sir, I know,' said the servant, 'but it's true. Mr Wickem, the clerk, has just brought the news on his way to ring the church bell. You'll hear it yourself in a moment. Listen! There it is.' And sure enough, the bell then began to ring, long and slow, telling the people of the village that someone had died.

Dr Hall stood up. 'This is terrible,' he said. 'I must go up to the Hall at once. The Squire was so much better yesterday. It seems so sudden.'

'Yes, sir,' agreed the servant. 'Mr Wickem said that the poor Squire was taken ill very suddenly with a terrible pain. He died very quickly, and Wickem said they want him buried quickly too.'

'Yes, yes; well, I must ask Mrs Bowles herself or Mr Joseph,' said the priest. 'Bring me my coat and hat, please. Oh, and tell Mr Wickem that I would like to see him when he has finished ringing the bell.' And he hurried off to the Hall.

When he returned an hour later, he found the clerk waiting for him.

'There's a lot of work for you to do, Wickem,' he said, 'and not much time to do it.'

'Yes, sir,' said Wickem. 'You'll want the family tomb opened, of course . . .'

'No, no, not at all,' replied Dr Hall. 'The poor Squire said before he died that he did not want to be buried in the family tomb. It is to be an earth grave in the churchyard.'

'Excuse me, sir,' said Wickem, very surprised. 'Do I understand you right? No tomb, you say, and just an earth grave? The poor Squire was too ill to know what he was saying, surely?'

'Yes, Wickem, it seems strange to me too,' said the priest. 'But Mr Joseph tells me that his father, or I should say his stepfather, made his wishes very clear when he was in good health. Clean earth and open air. You know, of course, the Squire had some strange ideas, though he never told me of this one. And there's another thing, Wickem. No coffin.'

'Oh dear, oh dear!' said Wickem. 'There'll be some talk about that. And I know that old Mr Wright has some lovely wood for the Squire's coffin – he's kept it for him for years.'

'Well,' said Dr Hall, 'those are the Squire's wishes, so I'm told, so that's what we must do. You must get the grave dug and everything ready by ten o'clock tomorrow night. Tell Wright that we shall need some lights.'

'Very well, sir. If those are the orders, I must do my best,' said Wickem. 'Shall I send the women from the village to prepare the body?'

'No, Wickem. That was not mentioned,' said the priest. 'No doubt Mr Joseph will send for them if he wants them. You have enough work to do without that. Good night, Wickem.' He paused. 'I was just writing out the year's burials in the church records. I didn't think that I'd have to add Squire Bowles' name to them.'

∝

The Squire's burial took place as planned. All the villagers and a few neighbours were present, and the Squire's stepson Joseph walked behind the body as it was carried to the churchyard. In those days nobody expected the Squire's wife to come to the burial. The Squire had no family except his wife and stepson, and he had left everything to his wife.

But what was everything? The land, house, furniture, pictures, and silver were all there, but no money was found. This was very strange. Squire Bowles was quite a rich man; he received plenty of money from his land every year, his lawyers were honest, but still there was no money. The Squire had not been mean with his money. His wife had all she needed, he sent Joseph to school and university, and he lived well. But still he earnt more money than he spent. Where was it?

Mrs Bowles and her son searched the house and grounds several times but found no money. They could not understand it. They sat one evening in the library discussing the problem for the twentieth time.

'You've been through his papers again, Joseph, have you?' asked the mother.

'Yes, Mother, and I've found nothing.'

'What was he writing the day before he died, do you know? And why was he always writing to Mr Fowler in Gloucester?'

'You know he had some strange ideas about what happens to a person's soul when he dies. He was writing to Mr Fowler about it but he didn't finish the letter. Here, I'll read it to you.'

He fetched some papers from the Squire's writing table and began to read.

My dear friend,

You will be interested to hear about my latest studies, though I am not sure how accurate they are. One writer says that for a time after death a man's soul stays close to the places he knew during life – so close, in fact, that he can be called to speak to the living. Indeed, he must come, if he is called with the right words. And these words are given in an experiment in Dr Moore's book, which I have copied out for you. But when the soul has come, and has opened its mouth to speak, the caller may see and hear more than he wishes, which is usually to know where the dead man has hidden his money.

Joseph stopped reading and there was silence for a moment. Then his mother said, 'There was no more than that?'

'No, Mother, nothing.'

'And have you met this Mr Fowler?'

'Yes. He came to speak once or twice at Oxford.'

'Well,' said the mother, 'as he was a friend of the Squire, I think you should write to him and tell him what . . . what has happened. You will know what to say. And the letter is for him, after all.'

'You're right, Mother,' replied Joseph. 'I'll write to him at once.' And he wrote that same evening.

In time a letter came back from Gloucester and with it a large packet; and there were more evening talks in the library at the Hall. At the end of one evening, the mother said:

'Well, if you are sure, do it tonight. Go round by the fields where no one will see you. Oh, and here's a cloth you can use.'

'What cloth is it, Mother?' asked Joseph.

'Just a cloth,' was the answer.

Joseph went out by the garden door, and his mother stood in the doorway, thinking, with her hand over her mouth. Then she said quietly, 'It was the cloth to cover his face. Oh, I wish I had not been so hurried!'

The night was very dark and a strong wind blew loud over the black fields; loud enough to drown all sounds of calling or answering – if anyone did call or answer.

Next morning Joseph's mother hurried to his bedroom. 'Give me the cloth,' she said. 'The servants must not find it. And tell me, tell me, quick!'

Her son, sitting on the edge of the bed with his head in his hands, looked up at her with wild, red eyes.

'We have opened his mouth,' he said. 'Why, oh why, Mother, did you leave his face uncovered?'

'You know how hurried I was that day,' she replied. 'I had no time. But do you mean that you have seen it?'

Joseph hid his face in his hands. 'Yes, Mother, and he said you would see it, too.'

His mother gave an awful cry and caught hold of the bedpost.

'He's angry,' Joseph went on. 'He was waiting for me to call him, I'm sure. I had only just finished saying the words when I heard him – like a dog growling under the earth.'

He jumped to his feet and walked up and down the room.

'And now he's free! What can we do? I cannot meet him again. I cannot take the drink he drank and go where he is! And I'm afraid to lie here another night! Oh, why did you do it, Mother? We had enough as it was.'

'Be quiet!' said his mother through dry lips. 'It was you as much as I. But why spend time talking? Listen to me. It's only six o'clock. Yarmouth's not far, and we've enough money to cross the sea – things like him can't follow us over water. We'll take the night boat to Holland. You see to the horses while I pack our bags.'

Joseph stared at her. 'What will people say here?'

'You must tell the priest that we've learnt of some of the Squire's money in Amsterdam and we must go to collect it. Go, go! Or if you're not brave enough to do that, lie here and wait for him again tonight.'

Joseph trembled and left the room.

❧

That evening after dark a boatman entered an inn at Yarmouth, where a man and a woman were waiting, with their bags on the floor beside them.

'Are you ready, sir and madam?' he asked. 'We sail in less than an hour. My other passenger is waiting by the boat. Is this all your luggage?' He picked up the bags.

'Yes, we are travelling light,' said Joseph. 'Did you say you have other passengers for Holland?'

'Just one,' replied the boatman, 'and he seems to travel even lighter than you.'

'Do you know him?' asked Mrs Bowles. She put her hand on her son's arm, and they both paused in the doorway.

'No,' said the boatman. 'He keeps his face hidden, but I'd know him again by his voice – he's got a strange way of speaking, like a dog growling. But you'll find that he knows you. "Go and fetch them out," he said to me, "and I'll wait for them here." And sure enough, he's coming this way now.'

❧

In those days women who poisoned their husbands were burnt to death. The records for a certain year at Norwich tell of a woman who was punished in this way, and whose son was hanged afterwards. No one had accused them of their crime, but they told the priest of their village what they had done. The name of the village must remain secret, because people say there is money still hidden there.

Dr Moore's book of experiments is now in the

University Library at Cambridge, and on page 144 this is written:

This experiment has often proved true – to find out gold hidden in the ground, robbery, murder, or any other thing. Go to the grave of a dead man, call his name three times, and say: 'I call on you to leave the darkness and to come to me this night and tell me truly where the gold lies hidden.' Then take some earth from the dead man's grave and tie it in a clean cloth and sleep with it under your right ear. And wherever you lie or sleep, that night he will come and tell you truly, waking or sleeping.

WORD FOCUS

Match each word with an appropriate meaning. Then use some of the words to complete the sentences below (one word in each gap).

cloth	the soft part of the ground, not rock or stone
coffin	making a low angry sound like a dog
earth	an important landowner in earlier times
experiment	a grave built of stone under or above the ground
grave (*n*)	to harm or kill a person by giving them food or drink which causes illness or death
growling	a hole in the ground in which a dead body is buried
hang	the part of a person that is believed to go on living after death
poison(ed)	a test done in order to see what happens
soul	a box in which a dead body is buried
squire	to kill someone by holding them above ground with a rope around the neck
tomb	a piece of any kind of material (e.g. cotton, wool)

1 The Squire did not want to be buried in the family _____. He wanted to be buried in an _____ grave.

2 The Squire was interested in what happens to a person's _____ when he dies.

3 Joseph took the _____ which was meant to cover the Squire's face when he was buried.

4 When Joseph was in the churchyard that night, he heard the Squire's voice _____ like a dog under the earth.

5 Joseph and his mother did not go to Holland – they returned to the village and told the priest that they had _____ the Squire.

STORY FOCUS

When Mrs Bowles and Joseph returned from Yarmouth that night, they went at once to talk to their priest, Dr Hall. Match Dr Hall's questions with Mrs Bowles's answers to make their conversation.

Dr Hall's questions:

1 'Mrs Bowles? Joseph? Why are you here? It's long past midnight.'

2 'But you were taking the boat from Yarmouth tonight, to collect some of the Squire's money in Amsterdam. Why didn't you go?'

3 '*Him?* Who? What are you talking about, Mrs Bowles?'

4 'Mrs Bowles, please try to be calm. Poor Squire Bowles is dead and buried. How could you possibly see him at Yarmouth?'

5 'Called him from his *grave!* How did you do that, Mrs Bowles?'

6 'And did Joseph see him? Did *you* see him, Mrs Bowles?'

7 'And why is he angry, Mrs Bowles? Can you tell me that?'

Mrs Bowles's answers:

8 'I'm talking about the Squire . . . my husband . . . he was there, waiting for us. It was horrible! Please help us, Dr Hall, please!'

9 'Dr Moore's book told us how to do it. Joseph took some earth from his grave, and slept with it under his right ear.'

10 'We've just come back from Yarmouth. We have to talk to you.'

11 'Because I murdered him. I gave him poison to drink, and I shall live in fear of him for the rest of my days . . .'

12 'Because we called him from his grave, Dr Hall. We wanted to ask him where he had hidden his money.'

13 'Yes, we were going to take the boat – and we went to Yarmouth, but we couldn't get on the boat because of . . . because of *him*.'

14 'I didn't see his face, but I heard his voice, like a dog growling. He sounded so angry, Dr Hall, and I'm so frightened.'

About the
Authors

~

EDGAR ALLAN POE

Edgar Allan Poe (1809–1849) was born in Boston, USA. His parents died when he was young, and he went to live with the Allan family in Richmond. He spent a year in university and then two years in the army. In 1831, he moved to Baltimore to live with his aunt and his cousin Virginia. For the next few years, life was difficult. He sold some stories to magazines, but they brought him little money. But he did find happiness with Virginia, whom he married in 1836.

From 1838 to 1844, Poe lived in Philadelphia, where he wrote some of his most famous horror stories. Then he moved to New York, where his poem, *The Raven*, soon made him famous. But Virginia died in 1847, and Poe began drinking heavily. He tried to kill himself in 1848 and died the following year.

Poe wrote many different kinds of stories, and his horror stories are only a small part of his work. But to most people the name Edgar Allan Poe means stories of death and madness, horror and ghosts.

SAKI

Hector Hugh Munro (1870–1916), the British writer known as Saki, was born in Burma (now known as Myanmar). After his mother died, he and his sister and brother went to live with their two aunts in England. Aunt Tom and Aunt Augusta hated each other and were not interested in children. So, like Conradin in *Sredni Vashtar*, Saki learned to dislike aunts and to dream of a world where animals were stronger than people and could punish them for being cruel and stupid.

In 1893 Saki joined the army in Burma, but became ill and returned to London three years later. He then worked as a journalist for *The Morning Post*, travelling in France, Poland, and Russia. When the First World War began, he joined the army, and was killed in France in 1916.

He is best known today for his short stories, which are both cruel and funny at the same time. He published five collections of short stories and two novels.

FREEMAN WILLS CROFTS

Freeman Wills Crofts (1879–1957) was born in Dublin, Ireland. His father died while he was still a child, and his mother married again. He was educated at colleges in Belfast, and at the age of eighteen he became a junior assistant engineer for a railway company. He had several jobs in railway engineering, and finally became Chief Assistant Engineer. While in this job, he wrote his first novel, *The Cask* (1920), which began his new career as a writer of detective fiction. In 1925 his first 'Inspector French' mystery was published, and he went on to write another twenty-nine novels about his favourite detective, including *Inspector French's Greatest Case* (1924). Because of the success of his novels, he was able to stop working and become a full-time writer.

As a railway engineer, Crofts used what he knew about trains and railways in many of his books and stories, and he was very good at mysteries involving timetables and alibis.

H. E. BATES

Herbert Ernest Bates (1905–1974) was born in Northamptonshire, England. His family were shoe-makers. After leaving school, he worked as a newspaper reporter and then in a shoe factory warehouse. He was often alone in the office, and this is where he wrote his first novel, *The Two Sisters*.

During the Second World War, Bates joined the Royal Air Force, and he also worked as the Armed Forces' first short-story writer. He wrote under the name 'Flying Officer X'. His most famous novel, *Fair Stood the Wind for France*, published in 1944, is about the crew of a British plane shot down in France. Bates also wrote about his war-time experiences in Burma.

For fifty years, Bates published at least one new novel or collection of short stories each year. He lived in the countryside of Kent, and like some of his characters, he is remembered as a passionate Englishman, with a deep love for the countryside and the beauty of nature.

THOMAS HARDY

Thomas Hardy (1840–1928) was born in a small village in Dorset, in the south of England. When he was a young man, he often played the fiddle at weddings and parties, and he loved listening to old people telling stories of country life. Later, Hardy put many of the characters and events from these stories into his own short stories and novels.

At twenty-two, he went to London to work as an architect, and there he started writing poems, stories, and novels. His fourth novel, *Far from the Madding Crowd*, was very popular, and from this he earned enough money to stop working, and also to get married. He wrote several other successful novels, but some readers did not like them, saying they were dark and cruel. After this, Hardy stopped writing novels and returned to poetry.

For most of his life, he lived in Dorset with his first wife, Emma. Soon after she died, he married again. After his death his heart was buried in Emma's grave.

ARTHUR C. CLARKE

Arthur Charles Clarke (1917–) was born in Somerset, England. From an early age he was interested in everything scientific, building his own wireless sets, telescopes to look at the moon, and several home-made rockets. He was also an enthusiastic reader and collector of science-fiction magazines.

In 1946 he published his first science-fiction short story, and two years later gained a degree in physics and mathematics from London University. Since 1956 he has lived in Sri Lanka, in a house full of computers and all kinds of modern electronic technology.

Arthur C. Clarke has written more than eighty books and five hundred articles and short stories. He has received many awards, and is famous both for his science writing – on space flight, scientific forecasting, and undersea exploration – and for his inventive and technologically detailed science fiction. All his life he has had a deep interest in the meeting point between science and science fiction. Many of his predictions have come true, and what is fiction today might easily become the fact of tomorrow.

M. R. JAMES

Montague Rhodes James (1862–1936) was born in Kent. He was a very clever student, and spent his life teaching and writing in two great colleges – King's College, Cambridge, and Eton College, a famous boys' school. He published many books and papers on his studies, and he only wrote about thirty ghost stories, but many people think he is one of the best writers of ghost stories that there has ever been. Many other writers have studied his stories carefully, and tried to make theirs as good.

James, known as 'Monty' to his friends, was not just a dry scholar. He was very popular with students, enjoyed the theatre, and used to read his own ghost stories out loud to his friends, while sitting by the fireside at Christmas. He was often asked if he believed in ghosts himself, but he was too clever a scholar to give a clear answer one way or the other. In the introduction to one of his books he wrote: 'Do I believe in ghosts? I am prepared to consider evidence and accept it if it satisfies me.'

READING CIRCLE ROLES

When you work on your role sheet, remember these words:

~ READ ~ THINK ~ CONNECT ~ ASK ~~ AND CONNECT

READ ~
- Read the story once without stopping.
- Read it again while you work on your role sheet.

THINK ~
- Look for passages in the story that are interesting or unusual. Think about them. Prepare some questions to ask about them.
- Think about the meanings of words. If you use a dictionary, try to use an English-to-English learner's dictionary.

CONNECT ~
- Connect with the characters' thoughts and feelings. Perhaps it is a horror story and we cannot 'connect' with an experience like this, but we can see how the characters are thinking or feeling.

ASK ~
- Ask questions with many possible answers; questions that begin with *How? Why? What? Who?* Do not ask *yes/no* questions.
- When you ask questions, use English words that everyone in your circle can understand, so that everyone can talk about the story.

AND CONNECT ~
- Connect with your circle. Share your ideas, listen to other people's ideas. If you don't understand something, ask people to repeat or explain. And have fun!

The role sheets are on the next six pages (and on page 113 there are role badges you can make). Bigger role sheets, with space for writing, are in the Teacher's Handbook. Or you can read about your role in these pages, and write your notes and questions in your own notebook.

Discussion Leader

STORY: _____

NAME: _____

The Discussion Leader's job is to . . .

- read the story twice, and prepare at least five general questions about it.
- ask one or two questions to start the Reading Circle discussion.
- make sure that everyone has a chance to speak and joins in the discussion.
- call on each member to present their prepared role information.
- guide the discussion and keep it going.

Usually the best discussion questions come from your own thoughts, feelings, and questions as you read. (What surprised you, made you smile, made you feel sad?) Write down your questions as soon as you have finished reading. It is best to use your own questions, but you can also use some of the ideas at the bottom of this page.

MY QUESTIONS:

1 _____

— _____

— _____

— _____

— _____

— _____

— _____

Other general ideas:

- Questions about the characters (*like / not like them, true to life / not true to life ...?*)
- Questions about the theme (*friendship, romance, parents/children, ghosts ...?*)
- Questions about the ending (*surprising, expected, liked it / did not like it ...?*)
- Questions about what will happen next. (These can also be used for a longer story.)

Summarizer

STORY: _____

NAME: _____

The Summarizer's job is to . . .

- read the story and make notes about the characters, events, and ideas.
- find the key points that everyone must know to understand and remember the story.
- retell the story in a short summary (one or two minutes) in your own words.
- talk about your summary to the group, using your writing to help you.

Your reading circle will find your summary very useful, because it will help to remind them of the plot and the characters in the story. You may need to read the story more than once to make a good summary, and you may need to repeat it to the group a second time.

MY KEY POINTS:

Main events:

Characters:

MY SUMMARY:

Connector

STORY: _____

NAME: _____

The Connector's job is to . . .

- read the story twice, and look for connections between the story and the world outside.
- make notes about at least two possible connections to your own experiences, or to the experiences of friends and family, or to real-life events.
- tell the group about the connections and ask for their comments or questions.
- ask the group if they can think of any connections themselves.

These questions will help you think about connections while you are reading.
Events: Has anything similar ever happened to you, or to someone you know? Does anything in the story remind you of events in the real world? For example, events you have read about in newspapers, or heard about on television news programmes.
Characters: Do any of them remind you of people you know? How? Why? Have you ever had the same thoughts or feelings as these characters have? Do you know anybody who thinks, feels, behaves like that?

MY CONNECTIONS:

1 _____

— _____

— _____

— _____

— _____

— _____

— _____

— _____

— _____

Word Master

W

STORY: _____

NAME: _____

The Word Master's job is to . . .

• read the story, and look for words or short phrases that are new or difficult to understand, or that are important in the story.
• choose five words (only five) that you think are important for this story.
• explain the meanings of these five words in simple English to the group.
• tell the group why these words are important for understanding this story.

Your five words do not have to be new or unknown words. Look for words in the story that really stand out in some way. These may be words that are:

• repeated often   • used in an unusual way   • important to the meaning of the story

MY WORDS	MEANING OF THE WORD	REASON FOR CHOOSING THE WORD
_____ PAGE_____ LINE _____		
_____ PAGE_____ LINE _____		
_____ PAGE_____ LINE _____		
_____ PAGE_____ LINE _____		
_____ PAGE_____ LINE _____		

Passage Person

STORY: _____

NAME: _____

The Passage Person's job is to . . .

• read the story, and find important, interesting, or difficult passages.
• make notes about at least three passages that are important for the plot, or that explain the characters, or that have very interesting or powerful language.
• read each passage to the group, or ask another group member to read it.
• ask the group one or two questions about each passage.

A passage is usually one paragraph, but sometimes it can be just one or two sentences, or perhaps a piece of dialogue. You might choose a passage to discuss because it is:

• important   • informative   • surprising   • funny   • confusing   • well-written

MY PASSAGES:

PAGE _____ LINES _____

REASONS FOR CHOOSING THE PASSAGE	QUESTIONS ABOUT THE PASSAGE

PAGE _____ LINES _____

REASONS FOR CHOOSING THE PASSAGE	QUESTIONS ABOUT THE PASSAGE

PAGE _____ LINES _____

REASONS FOR CHOOSING THE PASSAGE	QUESTIONS ABOUT THE PASSAGE

Culture Collector

STORY: _____

NAME: _____

The Culture Collector's job is to . . .

- read the story, and look for both differences and similarities between your own culture and the culture found in the story.
- make notes about two or three passages that show these cultural points.
- read each passage to the group, or ask another group member to read it.
- ask the group some questions about these, and any other cultural points in the story.

Here are some questions to help you think about cultural differences.

Theme: What is the theme of this story (for example, getting married, meeting a ghost, murder, unhappy children)? Is this an important theme in your own culture? Do people think about this theme in the same way, or differently?

People: Do characters in this story say or do things that people never say or do in your culture? Do they say or do some things that everybody in the world says or does?

MY CULTURAL COLLECTION (differences and similarities):

1 **PAGE** _____ **LINES** _____ : _____

_____

2 **PAGE** _____ **LINES** _____ : _____

_____

MY CULTURAL QUESTIONS:

— _____

— _____

— _____

— _____

PLOT PYRAMID ACTIVITY

A **plot** is a series of events which form a story. The Reading Circles **Plot Pyramid** is a way of looking at and talking about the plot of a story. The pyramid divides the story into five parts.

The Exposition gives the background needed to understand the story. It tells us who the characters are, where the story happens, and when it happens. Sometimes we also get an idea about problems to come.

The Complication is the single event which begins the conflict, or creates the problem. The event might be an action, a thought, or words spoken by one of the characters.

The Rising Action brings more events and difficulties. As the story moves through these events, it gets more exciting, and begins to take us toward the climax.

The Climax is the high point of the story, the turning point, the point of no return. It marks a change, for better or for worse, in the lives of one or more of the characters.

The Resolution usually offers an answer to the problem or the conflict, which may be sad or happy for the characters. Mysteries are explained, secrets told, and the reader can feel calm again.

HOW TO PLOT THE PYRAMID

1 Read your story again, and look for each part of the pyramid as you read. Make notes, or mark your book.

2 In your Reading Circle, find each part of the pyramid in the story, and then write down your ideas. Use the boxes in the diagram opposite as a guide (a bigger diagram, with space for writing in the boxes, is in the Teacher's Handbook).

3 Begin with the *Exposition*, and work through the *Complication*, the *Rising Action* (only two points), the *Climax*, and the *Resolution*.

4 Finally, your group draws the pyramid and writes the notes on the board, and then presents the pyramid to the class.

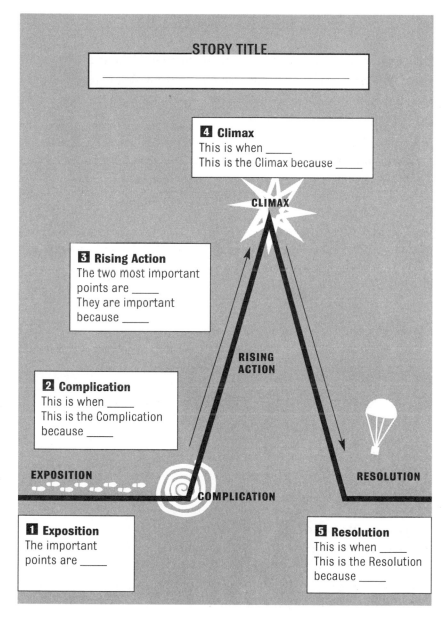

POSTER ACTIVITY

Each Reading Circle group makes a poster in English about a story in this book. Posters can have words, pictures, and drawings. Your group will need to find extra information about the story – perhaps from the Internet, or the school library, or your teacher.

Use the ideas on the opposite page to help you. When all the posters are finished, each Reading Circle will present their own poster to the other groups. At the end, keep all the posters, and make a 'poster library'.

STORY TITLE

THE THEME

What is the theme of the story?

• Is it about love or murder or friendship? Is it about dreams or wishes or fears?

THE TIME, THE PLACE

What do you know about the time and the place of the story?

• the city / the country?
• a real world, or an unreal world?
• If the time and place are not given, does it matter?

THE WRITER

What interesting facts do you know about the author's life?

• Was he or she also a poet, an actor, a teacher? Or a spy, a sailor, a thief, a doctor, a madman?

THE BACKGROUND

What cultural information did you learn from the story?

• About family events (for example, a wedding)
• A national holiday
• Family life (for example, parents and children)

THE LANGUAGE

What did you like about the language in the story?

• Find a quotation you like – words that are funny or clever or sad, or words that paint a picture in your mind.

THE FILM

Direct your own film! Who will play the characters in the film?

• Choose the best actors to play the characters.
• Where will you film it?
• Will you change the story?
• What title will the film have?

BOOKWORMS CLUB BRONZE
Stories for Reading Circles
STAGES 1 AND 2
Editor: Mark Furr

In these seven short stories there are marriages and murder, mistakes and mysteries. People fall in love, and fall out of love; they argue, and talk, and laugh, and cry. They go travelling, they go dancing – they even see ghosts. All of human life is here . . .

The Bookworms Club brings together a selection of adapted short stories from other Bookworms titles. These stories have been specially chosen for use with Reading Circles.

The Horse of Death
Sait Faik, from *Four Turkish Stories*

The Little Hunters at the Lake
Yalvac Ural, from *Four Turkish Stories*

Mr Harris and the Night Train
Jennifer Bassett, from *One-Way Ticket*

Sister Love
John Escott, from *Sister Love and Other Crime Stories*

Omega File 349: London, England
Jennifer Bassett, from *The Omega Files*

Tildy's Moment
O. Henry, from *New Yorkers*

Andrew, Jane, the Parson, and the Fox
Thomas Hardy, from *Tales from Longpuddle*

BOOKWORMS CLUB SILVER
Stories for Reading Circles
STAGES 2 AND 3
Editor: Mark Furr

In these seven short stories we find all kinds of people – a young couple in love, a clever young woman, a boy with an unhappy father, a madman, a famous detective, a daughter who stays out late, a man who cannot remember who he is . . .

The Bookworms Club brings together a selection of adapted short stories from other Bookworms titles. These stories have been specially chosen for use with Reading Circles.

The Christmas Presents
O. Henry, from *New Yorkers*

Netty Sargent and the House
Thomas Hardy, from *Tales from Longpuddle*

Too Old to Rock and Roll
Jan Mark, from *Too Old to Rock and Roll and Other Stories*

A Walk in Amnesia
O. Henry, from *New Yorkers*

The Five Orange Pips
Sir Arthur Conan Doyle, from *Sherlock Holmes Short Stories*

The Tell-Tale Heart
Edgar Allan Poe, from *Tales of Mystery and Imagination*

Go, Lovely Rose
H. E. Bates, from *Go, Lovely Rose and Other Stories*

ROLE BADGES

These role icons can be photocopied and then cut out to make badges or stickers for the members of the Reading Circle to wear.

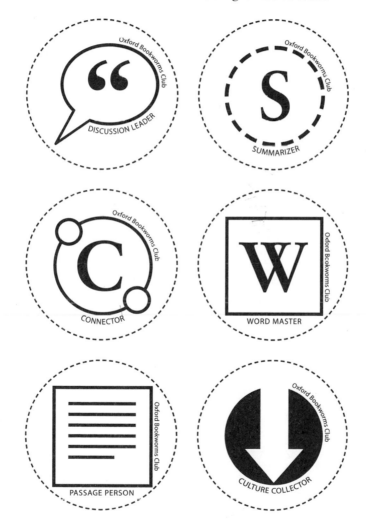